WITCH'S RITE

UNHOLY TRINITY BOOK 2

CRYSTAL ASH

PROLOGUE

DEJA

"Oh my God, Ash!" I gasped.

He laid on his back but I could see one of his wings peeking out from underneath him. What few white feathers remained were stained red with blood. The rest were charred or missing. And the angle of his wing seemed wrong, like the broken wing of a bird.

Only then did I notice the dark, tender bruises and welts on his side, wrapping around to his back. He looked as if he'd been burned, whipped, and pelted with rocks all at the same time.

But his eyes cracked open and he smiled at me like it was a typical, lazy Sunday morning.

"Hello, my love." His voice was gravelly with sleep as he reached for me.

"Ash, you're hurt!" I shrieked, too panicked to register his term of endearment.

"It's alright. Lucifer gave me something for the pain." He draped an arm across my waist and looked at me adoringly. "And with time, all will heal."

"But what happened?" I cried, hating that he'd been hurt so badly in the first place. I felt utterly helpless.

"We finally did it." He looked pleased, if a bit drugged out from whatever Lucifer gave him. "We rebelled. We took the fall. And I brought you with me."

"The fall?" I repeated as my mind scrambled to connect the dots.

"Yes, you're safe now." He reached for my hand and laced his fingers with mine. "No human man will ever make you submit to him again. You have all the same rights and powers as anyone else. All you have to do is take them."

As my thoughts raced, my eyes caught a mirror across from the bed and the reflection shocked me.

My eyes looked exactly the same golden-brown color. But other than that, I looked completely different. My hair was much longer, nearly down to my waist, and a coppery auburn color. With one glance down at my naked body, I saw I was much shorter and thinner. This was not the body I, Deja, was born in, and yet it was still mine.

"Lucifer suggests you form a legion to protect yourself," Ash continued in his lazy, sexy tone. "You won't be immortal like us but as the first human on our side, he will grant you powers over them." He eyed me curiously. "Or maybe he already has."

This had to be another one of my dream memories, right? There was no way I could wake up in a different body in a completely different place. But everything felt so real, from the sheets beneath me to Ash's arm wrapped around me.

And this raw power within me felt unmistakably real.

When I sat still and focused, I felt it traveling through me like millions of tiny high-speed trains. I closed my eyes and saw the Garden that was no longer my home. Yet still, wherever we were, I could draw the energy from the earth and will it to obey me.

"Turn over," I said abruptly. "Let me see your back."

Ash looked puzzled but obliged, rolling over on his stomach. I choked back a cry at what I saw. His injuries were far worse than I imagined. While the front of his torso was painfully beautiful and perfect, his back was a mess of deep gashes, mottled bruises, and painful welts. His left wing was a twisted deformity of broken bones with just a few feathers holding on. The right wing was gone completely, with a painful-looking, bloody hole where it once was.

If he were human, he simply would not have lived.

Steeling myself, I placed my palms carefully on his back and closed my eyes. I drew upon the resilient energy of the earth first up through my tailbone and collecting it in the center of my chest. I had no idea what I was doing, and yet I did. It was pure instinct.

I drew on the healing powers of nature, which always returned with a vengeance even when the last little leaf fell from the tree. From the center of my chest, I willed the magic of the natural world through my arms and out my palms. I willed for it to heal my lover, my savior, like it healed the earth. To take away his pain, and to give him great black wings fit for a ruler of Hell.

I didn't open my eyes for the longest time, too afraid to see if I failed him. But when I saw my palms pressed against smooth, flawless skin and rippling muscles, I collapsed with relief and joy.

"It worked!" Tears sprang to my eyes as I smoothed my hands across his back, unable to believe it. "You're healed!"

Ash sat up and checked the mirror, looking over his shoulder with adorable fascination. He stretched his majestic black wings carefully and my breath felt stolen from my body. I never saw a creature that looked so beautiful.

"I'll be damned," he breathed.

"Well, considering we're in Hell, you already are," I giggled.

"No, my love."

With an impish grin, he folded them against his back again and dropped on top of me. An explosion of love and warmth spread from my chest as he pulled me into a tight embrace and peppered my face with kisses.

"I'm not damned in the slightest, even if I am a demon now." He shifted to look at me with his crystal blue gaze. "Because of you, my love, I am truly blessed."

1

DEJA

"**F**ocus, Deja."

My grandmother's voice carried through me like a soothing breeze as I let out a deep breath, trying to clear my mind.

"Picture it in your mind and then say the words."

I concentrated hard on the image behind my eyelids, memorizing every small detail. I saw myself rooted to the ground like a tree, my arms extended like branches and whiplike vines growing from my fingertips.

As I focused, energy held me in place like an anchor while traveling up from the ground through my feet at the same time. It traveled through my veins like a river of heat and pure power.

The image in my mind nearly disappeared as the earth's magic surged through me but I held on, letting it coil up and build before I released it.

"Nothing gained, nothing lost," I said in a clear, commanding voice. "Life and death of equal cost. Here to grow, here to bleed. Leave this world and sow your seed."

My eyes shot open just as the magic exploded like gunshots from my fingertips, the force shooting back and making me stumble a few steps.

"It worked!" I shrieked triumphantly.

Long, green tendrils of magic sparkled like jade in the late afternoon sun as they wrapped around my target, a vase sitting on a coffee table across the room.

"Try to move it. Be gentle." My grandmother, Diana, contained her excitement better than me, but I still heard the pride in her voice.

I slowly waved my left hand and to my delight, the magic carried the vase in the exact direction I gestured. I rotated my wrist and the vase turned upside down in mid-air, a few drops of water spilling out.

"Try bringing it toward you," she suggested.

I moved my hands as if pulling on an invisible rope until the smoky green tendril held the vase directly in front of my chest.

"Well done, Deja," she praised. "You've truly improved by leaps and bounds."

"Thanks, Gran," I said as I directed the magic to return the vase to the coffee table. "You said I could use this spell on people too?"

"Yes, as long as you have enough magic manifested you can pick up and move mountains if you want to. But that takes a lifetime of practice," she chuckled before turning serious again. "This spell is ideal for restraining and subduing people without injury, if you ever find yourself in such a situation." She raised an eyebrow pointedly.

"Right," I nodded, chewing my lip. The last time I used magic on someone, I broke a guy's leg. To be fair, he was about to rape a girl so it wasn't like he deserved better. But at the time, I had just found out I was a witch and had zero training on how to channel my power. If I had somehow missed him and hit someone else, I'd have a much bigger problem on my hands.

"I wish your mother could see you now," Diana beamed as she lowered herself onto the couch, her stark white hair illuminating her face like a halo. "She was so excited to teach you the craft of our people."

I settled into the armchair across from her, picking up my teacup which had gone cold.

"Will you tell me about her?" I asked after some hesitation.

A week ago, Diana quite literally appeared at my

front door and told me a story that turned my life upside down. I had been adopted as a newborn to a deeply conservative religious couple. Growing up, I never felt like I truly belonged in my adoptive parents' world. Only after meeting Diana, my biological grandmother last week, did I learn that my birth mother was a witch and therefore, so was I.

My birth mother died soon after I was born under mysterious circumstances, although Diana was convinced that my deeply religious father made a deal with a demon to have her killed in order to protect his own reputation.

"She was always so happy," Diana began softly, smiling to herself. "So full of light. Deirdre saw the good in everyone and the upside in every bad situation. She was kind and gentle to every living creature, even ants that got into our kitchen. I know she would have been an excellent mother to you."

A wave of sadness filled me at the thought of such a beautiful person being taken away from this world. Someone I never got the chance to know and learn from. It felt wholly unfair that such a huge part of myself was kept hidden from me for so many years.

My adoptive parents, while they weren't cruel, believed my powers were a source of evil and did all they could to stifle my abilities with prayer and Bible study. In their own minds, they probably believed they were genuinely doing the right thing.

While I grew up never knowing my magical abilities, I always felt like an outcast in their tight bubble of a community. Moving to San Francisco was a culture shock in the best way, and finding out my witch heritage only solidified that I found my home in this big, magical city.

Better at twenty-eight years old than never, but I still couldn't help but mourn over what I never had-- a mother who raised me with love and acceptance. Someone who would encourage me and refine my gifts, not try to pray them away.

"Did you ever look into the details of her death?" I asked my grandmother, a spark of something lighting up within me. A sense of revenge? Justice? I couldn't be sure. "Find out who the demon was that my father paid? What exactly was the spell that killed her?"

Diana shook her head sadly.

"He steered clear of me because he was convinced I'd turn him into a toad or something. And legally he was her next of kin, so he made sure I never got too close to her or you in the end. He convinced the doctors and nurses I was crazy and would try to steal the baby. And if I knew he'd kill my daughter, I sure as hell would," she growled.

She leaned back tiredly in her armchair and rested her face in her hand, suddenly looking much older. Even with her stark white hair, her eyes were bright and her mind sharp. As I got to know her over the past week, I began to see more of my own features in her.

"No, my dear. I'm afraid it's just a mother's instinct and my own theory that the vile, hypocritical sperm donor hired a demon to do his dirty work. The magic surrounding her and you was so dark, darker than I'd ever seen. But trust me, it kills me every day not knowing for sure."

"There must be a way to find out though, right?" I asked, realizing I was latching onto finding the truth about my mother like a pit bull. "I mean, aren't there paranormal investigators or something like that?"

Diana laughed softly. "No, unfortunately we don't have anything like Scooby-Doo running around to solve these mysteries. Revealing ourselves to the non-magical authorities just poses too much of a risk."

"I get that but don't we have our own governing body? What if someone commits a crime with magic?"

"Problem witches are usually dealt with by their local covens. There are too few of us to have a real judicial system, unfortunately," she sighed. "We're lucky to have a sizeable witch population here in San Francisco."

I nodded my understanding but the gears inside my head turned like a well-oiled machine. For the sake of my stolen childhood and my mother's death, I was dying to find the missing pieces and click them into place. Maybe then I'd have some closure. And thankfully, I knew exactly who I'd ask my first questions.

"Thanks again for the lesson, Gran," I said, picking up our teacups with a quick glance at the clock. "I just might be getting the hang of this witch thing."

"Kicking me out already, eh?" she quipped teasingly, but I knew it wasn't a rhetorical question. "Got big plans for tonight, do you?"

"Sort of," I admitted, setting my teacups in the sink. "I found a bar downtown that's only visible by magic. Thought I'd check it out."

"Oh? By yourself?" Diana lifted a questioning eyebrow, making me squirm under her gaze.

"No, I'm uh, meeting someone there."

Or should I say *someones.*

"Oh really? Who?" My grandmother's questions burned into me, making me even more uncomfortable. For Christ's sake, I'd been living on my own and owning a business for over a year already. Maybe I was a little sheltered for my age but I wasn't a damn child.

But could I really blame her for being protective, since she couldn't be in my life until recently? Not to mention the fact that I was all that was left of her daughter, who was taken from her far too soon.

"Just some people I met," I said in an attempt to brush off her question. "I gotta make friends with more of my own kind, you know?"

"I see. So you've met some fellow witches?"

"Um, not exactly." I avoided her gaze as I squirmed even harder internally, wishing she would just let it go.

"Deja." She said my name in a low, warning tone as if scolding a child. "Are you seeing those demons you mentioned before?"

Fuck. Why was I such a terrible liar?

"We're just going to have some drinks and hang out," I said, sounding as if I was trying to convince myself as well as her that nothing else would happen. Especially since I had already made out with all three demons in question and found myself addictively attracted to them all equally.

Diana's lips pressed into a thin, tight line as her eyes narrowed at me. Her aura flared up with a silent anger that expressed her disapproval.

"Dear, please just promise me that you'll be careful," she pleaded. "It's true that demonkind have been unfairly portrayed throughout time but there is a seed of truth to every story. They are master manipulators and capable of wicked, awful things."

"So are humans," I answered defensively. "And witches too, I imagine."

"Yes, yes, of course," she said emphatically. "Just please use your best judgment and question everything they tell you. Don't take anything they say as absolute truth."

"I'll be careful, Gran," I assured her, wrapping her in a hug as we moved to the door. "I promise."

We said our goodbyes and I promised to be careful at least three more times before finally shutting the door after her. I couldn't help but feel a bad taste in my mouth as I finished tidying up my tea shop before leaving.

I realized she wanted to protect me. I was a fledgling witch still honing my powers, hanging out with creatures much older and more powerful than me. But she was of a different generation than me and her words felt eerily similar to an older white woman saying, "Well, I'm not racist, but..."

It didn't seem fair that she painted all demons with such a broad brush. Not that I knew many, only three. And barely at that.

They were all ridiculously hot though, and I seemed to have some kind of inexplicable bond between all of them. Nearly every night since I met them I've had extremely erotic dreams, vivid in every sense but sight. I could feel multiple hands and mouths pleasuring me like they were really there, but as if I were blindfolded. I wanted to say it felt like *them* but without even knowing, how could I be sure?

I smoothed my dark hair in the mirror and applied a fresh coat of lipstick. My reflection winked one amber eye back at me before I locked up and set out for the bar.

One of the core principles Diana taught me while using magic was to trust my instincts. For some reason, my gut felt more suspicious about her anti-demon rhetoric than the demons themselves. Every moment spent in their company made me feel I could trust them. But when she said things against them, my instinct was to rise up in their defense.

They knew something about me that I didn't, that maybe even my grandmother didn't know. Something that might explain how I felt so bonded and drawn to them after barely knowing them.

And possibly, more importantly, they might have some answers as to what happened to my mother.

2

DEJA

A brisk walk on a chilly San Francisco evening was never dull, especially not after discovering my magical abilities. After learning I was a witch, it was like awakening a sixth sense. I saw people's auras as I walked by them in a variety of colors, hues, and shapes. Some had small halos circling their head, others encompassed their whole body in an ethereal glow. I recently learned this was based on how strong their emotions were in that moment.

The discovery of my magic also led me to find actual, physical places that were invisible to ordinary humans, like my current destination, the Triple Moon pub.

When I first moved to San Francisco, I walked past this alley hundreds of times without a second glance. All I saw then were dumpsters and the backsides of buildings that faced the opposite street. But now the red brick building emitted a cozy, flickering glow from its windows as I hastily approached, eager to wrap my hands around a pint glass or maybe a whiskey tumbler. I hadn't decided yet.

I pulled the door open to a room full of warmth, laughter and many simultaneous conversations. The varnished wooden bar stretched out long before my eyes, lined with enchanted candles that never burned out or dripped wax. A massive chandelier mounted on the high, vaulted ceiling flickered with the same enchanting light. Across from the bar, couches, booths, and pub tables lent a few dim corners for privacy.

I didn't spot my demons right away, so I approached an empty space at the bar as I mused on what to drink.

"I'll have a sex on the beach, please," I said to the bartender. Why not. I was in a flirty mood.

"Is that a request?"

The question came from behind me while a large, heavy hand snaked around my hip at the same time, igniting my skin into delicious shivers.

I peered over my shoulder to find myself looking

up into a familiar pair of dark, mischievous eyes followed by a chiseled jaw coated in dark stubble, shoulder-length black hair, and a playful smirk on kissable lips.

"Even if it was, you'd have to whisk me away to Mexico or somewhere 'cause that ain't happening on the frozen, rocky shore here," I shot back at Raum.

The tall, dark, handsome demon's grin only grew wider as he squeezed my waist in a possessive grip that suggested we do exactly that. But you never really knew with Raum. He was like the Sphinx to Odysseus-- speaking in riddles, teasing, hinting, and never revealing all that he knew, which was a lot considering he could see the past and the future.

"Her drink is on my tab," he told the bartender, lacing his fingers through mine as he pulled me away from the bar. I could have swooned right then, but somehow kept my legs and drink steady as I followed him to a private corner with couches and a low table.

Sitting there, waiting for us was a man whose features were the polar opposite of Raum's, though no less breathtakingly handsome.

Where Raum was dark, flirtatious, and mysterious, Salmac was bright, blunt, and hotheaded. His sharp green eyes looked like a predatory cat in the flickering candlelight. His auburn hair, short on the sides and longer on top, shone with its own fire and luster. As for his clean-shaven, serious face? Well, I was essentially dying to kiss it.

"Hey Sal," I greeted, sliding into the booth and brushing a kiss against his cheek, too shy to initiate anything else.

He merely scoffed and cupped the nape of my neck, holding me in place as he delivered a hot, slow and sensual open-mouthed kiss that stole my breath away. His tongue probed my lips apart and confidently invaded me. When his mouth left mine, my brain buzzed like I had downed several drinks already.

"Hey beautiful," he murmured gruffly against my lips.

Well, that was one hell of a greeting. Something I could get used to.

"Now you're not going to let him have all the fun, are you?" Raum whispered against the shell of my ear.

I hadn't even recovered from the intoxication of Sal's kiss but turned to face Raum all the same. His mouth was waiting and captured mine in a kiss that was so deeply satisfying in such a different way. Sal's lips were soft and soothed an ache like a refreshing drink of water. Raum's stubble scratched roughly across my lips in the hottest, most spine-tingling way. His kisses also mirrored his teasing, flirtatious personality--biting my lips playfully before pulling away, leaving me begging for more.

My eyes remained softly closed as his mouth drew

away, not wanting to shatter the illusion that I just kissed two men within seconds of each other, and neither one of them seemed bothered by it.

"You're conflicted," came Sal's observant voice as a gentle touch brushed against my cheek. "I can feel it in your aura."

I opened my eyes to stare into the stunning green orbs of his, searching through me deeply. His intense gaze had to be intimidating to some, but it only filled me with warmth.

"I just don't understand how you all can be okay with this." I mused, looking over my shoulder at Raum before a realization dawned on me. "And where's Ash?"

"Hell," Raum answered as casually as if he said the word, *work*. "Business with Beelzebub and Lucifer. He'll be back in a day or so."

Ash, or Ashtaroth, the leader of these devilishly handsome musketeers, was a fallen angel and one of the original founders of Hell. And as far as I could tell, the most mysterious and stoic of the three. He exuded immense power but with a cool and aloof nature, unlike Sal's hot-headedness. In contrast to Raum's joking and teasing nature, Ash was quiet and serious.

Also, he was the first one to kiss me.

Even with Sal and Raum here to keep me company, I realized I missed him.

With Sal's hand still gently stroking my cheek and neck, Raum wrapped a muscular, corded arm around my waist. The sensation of both touches was nearly overwhelming, but in the most affectionate way that sent butterflies through my insides.

"And we're okay with this because we're not bound by dogmatic social constructs deeply rooted in patriarchal Christianity," Raum added, a naughty glimmer in his eye.

"But the real question is," Sal chimed in. "Are *you* okay with this?"

"I... like all three of you," I answered, pausing in my nervousness to take a sip of my sex on the beach. "But I don't even know what *this* is." My eyes darted between the two of them. "Are you all doing this with other people?"

"No," they answered in unison. The conviction in their voices both put me at ease and lit a fire inside me. So all three of them wanted just me and no one else? It seemed too good to be true.

"I wish we could just tell you everything. All the history between us," Sal sighed, looking longingly at my lips. "But Ash is insistent that you figure it out for yourself."

"It probably is better that way," Raum added. "It's a lot of very heavy information to digest, especially since you're still getting used to the idea that you're not an ordinary human."

"Well, all this vaguebooking and obscure references

is certainly helping," I remarked sarcastically, taking a long pull from my drink.

"Oh but isn't solving your own mystery part of the fun?" Raum teased, rubbing circles on my lower back. "What have you deduced so far, Nancy Drew?"

I sipped more of my fruity, flirty cocktail as I pondered his question, hyper-aware of their eyes on me as I sucked the straw and my cheeks hollowed in.

"You're all ancient compared to me," I began. "And yet you all act as if you know me from before my own lifetime. Since meeting you all and discovering my powers, I have felt... comfortable. At ease. Even familiar, like I've met you all before, too. So I can only deduce that I must be some sort of reincarnation of... someone."

"Very good," Raum purred, sounding pleased.

"Wait, what?" I said, taken aback. "You mean I'm right? Like reincarnation is real?"

"Perhaps not in the exact same sense you're thinking but yes, a person's true self can be reborn in another body after the first one dies. It's just as real as magic is," he answered with a wily smile.

"And I've done that before," I thought out loud.

"Yes," they both agreed.

"But is it like this every time?" I wondered. "Where I live my life like an ordinary person and then meet you for the first time and you all have to drop these hints until I figure it out? Like some kind of long drawn-out, fucked up Groundhog Day?"

In my frustration, my hands gestured wildly in the air as I spoke, until dropping onto both Sal and Raum's thighs pressed against me in the booth. A hot jolt shot up through me and I resisted the urge to pull my hands away like I touched a burning stove.

Lord help me. Or should I say, Satan *help me.*

"No, it's not supposed to be like this," Sal murmured mournfully, lacing his fingers through mine on his leg. "You don't remember any of your past lives? Or your original name?"

I shook my head slowly, my heart aching at the sadness and loss in his eyes. Whoever I had been, he really missed me and it hurt him that I didn't remember. His words from our two truths and a lie game rang through my head-- *I've been in love with the same woman for over seven thousand years.*

3

DEJA

It wasn't until opening my tea shop the next morning, after a nice buzz of caffeine, that I realized I forgot all about asking the guys questions related to my mother.

"Damn it," I muttered into my third cup of lavender chai.

"What's up?" asked Nona, my only employee. I swore she had the hearing of an elephant.

"Nothing. Just got a fly in my cup," I muttered as I turned toward the sink.

I felt guilty for keeping all my witchy developments a secret from Nona. She wasn't just my employee but my first and only real friend since moving out to San Francisco.

I stepped off that Greyhound bus a sheltered and naive girl, the perfect prey for a fast-paced, cutthroat big city to swallow up whole and spit out in pieces.

I didn't even make it out of the bus terminal before someone mugged me. If she hadn't ridden her bike past me at that exact moment and saw the whole thing, I could have spent my first night sleeping on the side-walk. It was serendipitous. She never left my side again after that.

Even though she worked for me, she was like a mother figure in many ways, like gently reminding me when rent was due, and where the best Mexican food and bars were.

Hell, she even encouraged me to hook up with all three demons after we first met them at that party. That was before either of us knew they were demons, of course.

I hated lying to her. In fact, I was bursting to tell her everything. I needed a girl friend-- who was not my grandmother-- to confide in.

Simple logic told me it was unwise to tell non-magical humans about my powers. Diana hinted at that when we talked about paranormal investigators last night. If knowledge of our powers fell into the wrong hands, it could be devastating.

But this was my sweet Nona. I would bet my life on

her loyalty and trustworthiness. Would it really be so bad if I told her I broke a man's leg without touching him? And that the devilishly handsome guys I liked were *actual* demons?

Something in the air suddenly pulled my attention like a magnet. I looked out across the tea shop to see a young woman sitting by the window, an Earl Grey latte on the table in front of her and a book in her hand.

My eyes narrowed as I tried to make out the title of the book. The jacket certainly looked familiar.

I nearly dropped my cup when I realized it was one of the same spellbooks Diana had been teaching me from, *The Magical Properties of Plants* by Alastair Knowles.

My heart jumped into my throat as I blocked out everything else in the shop and focused on this young woman with serious tunnel vision.

She looked about my age with pale blonde hair down her back in pretty waves. Her large eyes were a brilliant aquamarine color, and a large chunk of raw crystal in a similar color hung around her neck on a long chain.

Her aura shimmered around her whole body in the same brilliant bluish-green color, with slow, undulating movement like the way a mermaid tail would swim through water. Essentially, she looked bathed in the brilliant lights of the Aurora Borealis.

And she was most definitely a witch.

Only then did I glance around, to see if any other patrons noticed this woman bathed in ethereal light and reading from a spellbook. But everyone chatted with friends, worked on laptops, read ordinary books, and sipped their tea as if nothing was amiss.

"Hey Nona," I said as casually as I could muster. "Has that girl in the window been in here before?"

"No, I don't think so," she said just as casually, pulling cups and saucers out of the dishwasher.

"Have you uh, noticed what she's reading?"

Nona paused and took a longer glance.

"A chemistry textbook, huh? Heavy subject matter. She's probably a student."

I blinked and bit my tongue before I could reveal my shock. I looked again and sure enough, the book cover now read *Organic Chemistry*.

I'll be damned. Disguising the book with magic. So simple but genius.

To anyone looking, I was a calm shop owner sipping my tea while looking out adoringly at my customers. But on the inside, I was a twisted mess of anxiety and excitement, like a high school girl debating on saying "hi" to her crush.

Should I talk to her? What should I even say? Oh hi, nice to meet another witch for the whole shop to hear? Do witches have some kind of code word or secret handshake?

Damn it Deja, just leave the girl alone. Like everyone

else in here she probably just wants to read her book and drink tea in peace.

...But what if she's like me and is desperate for someone to talk to about witchy things?

Her aquamarine eyes lifted from her book and caught mine from across the room.

Fuck! I'd been staring at her like a creep for who knows how long.

I abruptly turned and drained the last of my chai, staring intently at my cash register for a distraction.

The door then jingled with a new customer walking in and I looked up with a bright, plastered smile, grateful for an actual distraction and boy, did I get one.

"Ash!" I gasped as my heart crashed against my ribs and my body temperature rose with every passing second.

"Deja," the fallen angel greeted me huskily as he approached the counter, turning a few heads as he did so.

With his tall, imposing form exuding raw power that even ordinary humans could sense, such reactions couldn't be helped.

His icy blue eyes froze me to my spot but the way he looked at me set my body on fire. He stroked his short, blonde beard as he approached me and gave the barest hint of a smile on his stony face. His blonde hair was tousled carelessly. I wanted nothing more than to run my hands through it and mess it up even more.

"Where've you been?" I asked more eagerly than I intended.

He braced his muscular forearms on my counter and leaned down slowly, deliberately, to my level.

"A bit busy. Just putting out some fires," he said, his low voice rumbling like lazy thunder.

"Literal or figurative fires?" I asked, lifting an eyebrow.

"A bit of both," he replied, never breaking his intense gaze from mine.

Like Sal and Raum, Ash's aura was incredibly dark with sparks of red and crackles of electricity. Of the three of them, he was the only one who also had large black wings sprouting from his back. Ordinary humans couldn't see them, but I wondered if the aquamarine witch noticed them.

I glanced up to her window and was surprised to see she was gone.

"Did you have fun with Sal and Raum last night?"

Ash's question jerked my attention back to him along with a tightening in my throat.

"You can tell me honestly," he said in a way that was oddly gentle and soothing. "The three of us hide nothing from each other."

I swallowed. "Yes," I admitted. "I did have a nice time with them."

"Good." His eyes flashed. "I ordered them to take care of you while I was away."

"It was just drinks and kissing," I stammered. "We didn't--"

"I know, Deja." His hand slid across the counter to brush against mine. The heat of his touch calmed my panic.

I took a deep breath, trying to maintain control of myself with my body getting so hot and the chemistry visibly crackling between us.

"So what can I do for you, Ash?" I said. "Seeing as you're not a tea person."

"Come home with me," he said without missing a beat.

"What?"

"I missed you, Deja." His index finger drew some invisible gesture on the sensitive skin inside my wrist. "I was only gone for a day here but time passes much more slowly in Hell. It feels like I haven't seen you in weeks."

My heart squeezed in my chest. The words tumbled out of me before my brain could catch up.

"It felt the same way to me."

4

DEJA

I couldn't bring myself to leave work early, no matter how hotly Ash stared at me or how badly I wanted to see what a naked demon really looked like. It wouldn't be fair to Nona, making her close up on her own.

But that didn't make the afternoon pass any faster.

"I'll hang out if you don't mind," Ash said at my insistence at staying until closing. "I like the feel of your space here."

"Sure," I said calmly while I internally squealed with excitement. "I'd offer you something to drink but, you know." I waved my hand dismissively at him.

Yeah, I was giving him shit for not being a tea

person and probably would be for the foreseeable future.

At least Raum liked my tea. I still had yet to get Sal's opinion.

"If you give me a cup, I'll handle the beverage part myself," he said with a wink.

I gave him a quizzical look but handed him a freshly washed teacup anyway. Like a magician, he passed his hand over the rim and the cup was suddenly filled with a dark, steaming liquid. A familiar, earthy smell filled my nostrils.

"Coffee, really?" I said. Not exactly what I expected to be conjured out of thin air.

He shrugged as he brought the hot liquid to his lips and took a small sip. "Just my poison of choice."

"I see. And you take it black, I imagine?"

"As black as my soul," the handsome demon confirmed with a smirk.

I didn't doubt him for a second.

He produced a worn-out looking book in his other hand and nodded toward an empty armchair.

"I'll be out of your way, Deja," he said. "Until we can leave," he added in a lower tone.

I tried not to ogle as he settled himself with his book and coffee in my tea shop. Before long, every woman was stealing glances at him and I couldn't blame them. He looked so studious, like the hot, slightly nerdy professor that everyone had a crush on in college.

"Something tells me Mr. Hot Blonde is waiting for you to leave work," Nona teased as the minutes crawled by.

"Yeah," I said, my face heating up as I tried to concentrate on the current brew. "We might be hanging out afterward."

"Hanging out as in romantic dinner or Netflix and chill?"

"Um, kind of sounds like the second one."

"Ooh, get it, girl!" She bumped into me with the side of her hip.

"And you didn't hear this from me but um." I chewed my lip nervously. "I may have made out with the two other guys last night."

Nona's mouth dropped open. "Girl."

"And they all apparently know about each other and are okay with everything."

"Girl!"

"It sounds way too good to be true but they say they're all interested in just me."

I didn't know why I started spilling all these private details to her, they just came pouring out. I figured I could talk to her about my love life but just leave the supernatural details out.

"Holy shit, Deja you've hit the holy grail of jackpots!

Ride this out for as long as you can. Or should I say, ride all *three* of them."

"Geez, Nona! Why not say it loud enough for the whole shop to hear," I hissed, looking over both of my shoulders.

At some point, Ash put on a pair of thick-rimmed reading glasses and I had to bite my lip to stifle a moan.

"Oh chill out, Deja. Nobody in San Francisco cares how many people you sleep with. Hell, you could even throw another girl into the mix and no one will bat an eye."

"Yeah, that is definitely not happening," I muttered, stealing yet another glance at Ash.

He seemed deeply absorbed into his book, his brows pinching together slightly as his pale blue eyes moved over the words. A couple of girls at a nearby table whispered to each other as they kept looking at him. A different kind of fire heated my blood. I hoped they weren't planning on talking to him.

"Don't worry, your three devilishly hot men will corrupt your brainwashed upbringing in no time," Nona teased.

"You have no idea how much I can't wait for that," I replied.

5

DEJA

Closing time finally came and I didn't have to murder any of my female customers.

Ash said a polite goodbye to Nona before I finally shooed her away and locked up the shop. She barely rode her bike down the street before I received a text saying, "You better tell me everything!"

I rolled my eyes but held back a goofy grin as I stuck my phone in my purse and began walking along Ash's side.

"So what was with the readers?" I asked as we came to our first stoplight, and couldn't help but tease him. "Getting a bit old, are we?"

He cast a cheeky sideways glance at me. "My

eyesight is actually improving the longer I stay on earth. But yes, I used to be extremely farsighted and couldn't see anything in front of my face for the first hundred or so years after falling. I imagine it has to do with angels having to see across long distances from the clouds."

"Sort of like birds of prey," I mused aloud.

"Yes, exactly," he confirmed. "Binocular vision, they call it."

It was hard for my brain to wrap around the fact that this devastatingly handsome, but otherwise normal looking man walking next to me, was a not a human but a completely different creature.

And so was I, in a way.

"Do other demons have that problem?" I asked.

"Only the fallen angels, which are by far a minority. For the others, it depends on how they were created. Though eyesight problems aren't usually part of the package."

"Oh," I said. "I guess I assumed all demons were fallen angels."

"A common myth purported by Christ's followers," he said slyly. "No, Sal was created in Hell, for example. He is a manifestation of basic human and animal instincts like the need to conquer, dominate and protect."

"That makes sense." I remembered Sal's temper, which was never directed at me, but he always seemed eager to annihilate someone for even sending a dirty look my way. In his thousands of years of existence, he must've annihilated scores of enemies. I was beyond glad to be on his good side.

"And Raum was originally a raven. One of the first birds we observed that demonstrated incredible intelligence and almost human-like thought processes. When we saw him steal treasure from greedy kings, we knew we had to make him our own. He has excellent near and farsightedness, the bastard."

"Seriously?" I nearly stopped in my tracks. "Raum is actually a bird?"

"He was," Ash corrected. "He's a demon now. He actually prefers to spend most of his time in human form."

"Easiest for him to talk shit that way," I joked.

"Precisely," Ash chuckled. "There are also the lesser demons such as the incubi and the succubi. Each of us has a few legions of those under our command at any given time. Aside from immortality, their only real power is sexual seduction."

"That's it?"

He nodded. "Appealing to instinctual desires is one of the simplest, most effective ways to corrupt. If a human has been sexually shamed or repressed for most of their life, that often makes it easier."

"How so?" I asked, hanging onto his every word with fascination.

"When you ignore your instincts for so long, they don't go away," he said, his fingertips applying light pressure to my spine. "They're held by a hair trigger just below the surface, waiting for the one thing that'll set off the control they cling to so desperately. The seducing demons can identify the trigger and become exactly what that person desires most."

"That's fascinating," I mused. "Do all demons have seductive powers like that?"

"Not as much as the succubi, but to some extent." His fingers trailed down my arm to tug at my hand. "This is us." He led me up the front steps of a classic Victorian-style house painted a dark grey with an off-white trim.

He opened the front door for me to a dark, nearly pitch black foyer. Only tiny slivers of light came through the cracks between the blackout curtains on the windows.

An herbal, smokey smell filled my nostrils like some kind of incense, but all I could see were rough shapes of furniture, walls, and a staircase.

"Let me guess," I said, blinking in the darkness. "You three are vampires, too? Actually no, don't tell me that. I don't think I can handle any more mind-blowing revelations."

Ash's throaty chuckle came from somewhere behind me.

"No, we're not vampires." His warm breath lifted the

hairs on the back of my neck. "Just ensuring we have some privacy."

He snapped his fingers and I jumped at the sudden *whoof* sound that followed. The large brick fireplace roared to life with a nearly bonfire-sized flame, bathing the living room in warmth and a dancing, romantic light.

Although my heart thumped wildly in my chest, I kept my face neutral.

"Show off," I jabbed at his smug expression.

"Me? Never." His powerful arms wrapped around my waist, securing me against his hard chest. "You must be thinking of Raum."

The air between us was the thickest it had ever been. Our auras crackled with tension, the colors blending and practically kissing each other above both of our heads.

"No," I whispered. "I'm not thinking of him."

He leaned down to close the distance between us but stopped, pausing just before making contact. So I closed the gap for him.

I stood on tiptoe to reach his lips and felt some kind of combination of melting and exploding on the inside. He let out a soft grunt at my boldness but kissed me back. We fell into the same hot rhythm of teeth and tongue like that first time in the back of my shop.

We parted breathlessly and too soon. I was too hot and had too much clothing on.

"So you do want this as much as I do," he murmured against my lips.

"Yes," I breathed as I clutched to him desperately, fearing my legs wouldn't work if I let go.

Still he pulled back, holding me trapped under the icy fire of his gaze.

"There's something you should know before we do this," he said in a low growl.

"Okay?" I said, already panting with need.

"Here's the thing about me, Deja." His gaze flickered down to my lips and then back to my eyes. "I'm not jealous, I'm possessive. You can fuck Raum and Sal whenever you want. But when you're with me?" He wound his fingers through my hair and closed his fist at the base of my skull in a possessive grip.

"It's no one else but us."

He lowered his forehead to mine and gave the slightest, sweeping kiss over my flushed, trembling lips.

"Are you okay with that arrangement?" he asked in a way that sounded like a dare.

My brain and body were too delirious to answer in words, so I just kissed him again. Hard.

Wanting me all to himself yet still willing to share? It was like a paradox that I couldn't handle but made me so incredibly hot.

His tongue surged into my mouth as he pulled me

against him so tightly, I gasped for air but still couldn't get enough of him.

I felt so drunk on how badly I wanted him, my feet didn't even feel like they were on the ground anymore. I was in freefall.

When something soft but firm supported my back, I realized my feet did come off the ground. He picked me up and laid me down on the shag rug in front of the fire.

My core pulsed with a dull, aching need as he gently settled his weight on top of me, my thighs glued to the outside of his hips and pulling him toward my center.

"Li--, ah, Deja," he groaned hotly into my neck as one adventurous hand explored under my shirt.

I froze, barely catching it in my lust-filled haze, but it was enough to kill everything for me. My hooded eyes snapped open and my body went stiff, no longer melting against his. He noticed immediately and reluctantly pulled his mouth away to look at me.

"Something wrong?"

"Please tell me you didn't almost just call me by someone else's name," I said, trying to keep the emotion out of my voice.

"What? No," he protested but his face gave him away. "Deja, I--"

"Liar," I said, pushing up on his broad shoulders. "Get off me."

After wanting nothing more than to feel him inside me, I suddenly felt the complete opposite-- shitty, used, humiliated, and dying to get away. I had to leave before he saw me cry.

He sat up slowly. I quickly adjusted my clothes and scooted out from under him.

"Wait," he growled, catching hold of my wrist before I could stand. "Please listen to me."

"Let me go," I hissed, the tears already threatening to spill.

"That wasn't another person's name, it was yours," he said quickly. "I almost said the name you had when I first met you."

He released his hold on me and for some reason, I stayed rooted to my spot.

"Not in this lifetime but when I fell," he went on. "The *very* first time."

A light bulb went on somewhere in the back of my mind. So the reincarnation theory really was true. Apparently, I had been alive since nearly the beginning of time itself. All the feelings of familiarity and deep bonds with these men started making sense.

But at that moment, my pride was wounded and I did not want to let him off the hook.

"So what was it?" I challenged. "What was my name back then?"

He leaned his head back and sighed, looking conflicted.

"I can't tell you. I'm sorry."

"How convenient," I muttered, rising to my feet and heading toward the door.

"Pay attention to your dreams," he called after me. "The answers are there."

I paused with my hand on the doorknob and one foot outside.

"What do you mean?"

In a split second he stood next to me, icy blue eyes hungry and full of desire.

"The dreams you have. They feel like memories because they are. The more time you spend with us and the more physical contact we have, the more you remember. You have to remember yourself, Deja. We can't just sit you down and tell you. It could... affect your memories and perceptions."

He bit his lip, looking conflicted for a moment before he spoke again.

"One thing I can tell you is you're the only one for me. You always have been, since the beginning. Raum and Sal will undoubtedly tell you the same." His gaze lowered to my lips. "There has never been anyone else. No other name is even worth saying."

6

_____

DEJA

I saw someone in a dream that night who looked like Ash, yet so completely different.

His face was clean shaven and his blonde hair grew out in curls to his collarbone, but his icy, curious eyes were the same.

Most impressively, he shined with a brilliant light and had an amazing span of pure, white wings stretching out from his back.

"Who are you?" I asked.

"I am Ashtaroth, an angel of our Lord," he answered.

Distantly, I knew this was the first time we met. This was not a dream but a memory.

I remembered falling in love with that handsome face the moment I saw him. Those eyes sought knowledge and companionship, not obedience. In them, I saw freedom and escape from my situation, a man who essentially wanted to keep me as a slave.

I opened my mouth to tell him my name. He probably already knew it but this time *I* would know. One small piece of the big, blank puzzle of my past would fall into place.

But when my lips parted, all that came out was, "Beep! Beep! Beep!"

"Son of a fucking bitch!"

My hand shot out to my nightstand and sent the beeping alarm clock crashing to the floor. If I had been any more awake, I would have picked it up and thrown it across the room.

"What the fuck, man? Ugh!" I groaned in frustration into my pillow, pounding my fists and kicking my legs like a child.

I almost fucking had it. At this point, I was well and truly sick of this game. Fuck these demon boys and their, "Oops, we can't tell you anything," bullshit. I was going to make them stop jerking me around if I had to grab them by their damn demon balls to do it.

I launched out of bed and got ready to open the tea shop, which was conveniently located right below my apartment. At that moment however, I could have used a brisk walk up and down some of San Francisco's hills to blow off this steam.

But there was no time. I stomped downstairs to find Nona already decanting the overnight cold brews.

"Morning! Those were here for you when I opened." She gestured across the counter to a bouquet of roses in a slim, glass vase.

And no ordinary roses. While their petals were fresh, they were as black as ink, with Ash's aura hanging all around them like a perfume cloud. The sight of them made my anger soften. Just a tiny bit.

"So, how did it go last night?" She turned to me, wiggling her eyebrows but immediately stopped when she saw my expression. "That bad, huh?"

"Not exactly," I muttered, folding a pile of clean tea towels. "The night ended before anything could actually happen."

"Okay, be honest," Nona said before lowering her voice to a whisper. "Small dick?"

"Didn't even get that far," I replied, averting my gaze. "I'm not really in the mood to talk about it."

"Aw, that's a shame," she commiserated. Then in a much chirpier voice, "Good morning! What can we get started for you?"

I looked up to find myself staring into a brilliant aquamarine gaze. My heart stopped in my chest and I froze like a statue. It was the witch from yesterday!

"I'll take a pot of the dragon's blood blend," she said in a high, musical voice and with a sweet smile.

Nona scurried off to prepare her teapot, leaving me at the counter to stare at her dumbly.

She cleared her throat and rummaged in her purse.

"Um, it's five dollars, right?"

"Yes!" I declared, blinking out of my trance and swiftly moving to the register. "How's your morning so far?"

"Good, thanks," she replied politely. "How's yours?"

"Just... *magical*."

"Great."

Her aura flickered with a shimmering shift from green to blue, but her expression didn't twitch in the slightest as she handed over a five.

"So you're the owner?" she mused casually.

"Yes!" I stuck my hand out so abruptly I nearly poked her in the sternum. "I'm Deja."

"Juno," she answered, taking my hand in a gentle grip. "I love coming to this place. It's so relaxing."

"Thank you, it's great to have you." I forced myself to let go of her hand, despite a pleasant hum of energy passing through our palms. "Just let me know if you need anything."

"I sure will," she said, picking up the tray with the teapot, cup, and mini breakfast scone that Nona had swiftly set down. "Nice to meet you, Deja."

"You too, Juno."

I stretched and clenched my fingers as I watched her set her tray down on a coffee table and began thumbing through a book.

She did something magical when she touched my hand but it was so subtle, I didn't even know if I should acknowledge it or not. It felt too light to be an actual spell. Could that have been the secret witch handshake?

She sat at an angle where I couldn't read her book cover this time, but her wrist flicked and her fingers moved in a subtle but unmistakable way. I fought the urge to launch myself over the counter and pick her brain, to find out what she was casting and learn it for myself.

Screw the demon boys. They were not my priority, at least not at that moment. Growing my powers, and finding a community with others like me, was.

7

RAUM

A morning flight had been a daily ritual of mine for the last three hundred years or so. Watching the human world wake up was always fascinating, and always shifting depending on the time period and location.

I noticed humans were slowly rising later in the day, sometimes missing dawn entirely. Their workdays shifted further back. First, it was sunup to sundown, then it was nine to five. Lately, I noticed more ten to six schedules, especially in San Francisco where everyone wanted to skip morning traffic.

Yes, I gathered lots of useless knowledge in my bird

form. But you never knew when it would turn out to be useful.

After a few hours of fighting with seagulls and watching runners on the beach as the sun came up, I flew back to the house we occupied while in human form.

Through the open window I usually came through, I spotted Ash pacing in the upstairs study. He looked even more grim than usual.

I flapped and braced for landing, gripping the windowsill in my claws. Behind Ash stood Sal, staring at Ash like he wanted to kill him and holding the edge of a chair in a death grip.

"Seems I missed a cheerful morning meeting," I said after shifting back to human form.

"This fucking hypocrite almost told Deja her original name," Sal hissed through gritted teeth. "After being all up our asses constantly about not telling her shit."

I lifted an eyebrow. "Is that so, boss?"

"It is," Ash said tersely, not one to mince words. "But I didn't say it. I caught myself."

"Clearly, you said enough if Sal is so riled up."

"He gets riled up by the wind blowing the wrong way," Ash scoffed.

"Fuck you! Why don't you tell him the rest of it?" Sal seethed. His aura grew and flames began to ignite all around him like his skin was burning.

Ash looked at me. "You already know, don't you?"

"She thought you were going to call her by someone else's name," I said with a nod. "I felt her pain and embarrassment. It felt like a betrayal."

Ash's tight-lipped frown and the regret in his eyes confirmed it.

"It was a misunderstanding," he said. "I explained myself and I think she believed me. But I still planted seeds of doubt in her mind."

"This is fucking why we should just tell her," Sal declared. "She must think this is such a mind game and we're just jerking her around. Nearly a thousand years of waiting for our woman to come back to us and we might lose her because of *you*."

"You think I don't fucking know that?"

Ash whipped around to face Sal, who tossed the chair aside like it was a tennis ball. It crashed into the wall in a shower of splinters that forced me to shield my eyes. When I looked again they were nose-to-nose like a pair of boxers facing off, both brimming with explosive energy.

"This is precisely why we shouldn't say anything, so we don't allow for more misunderstandings," Ash snarled with aggression that was rare to see from our cool, aloof leader. "So I lost my head for a second and fucked up. I'm not an angel anymore, in case you forgot."

"What is there to misunderstand if we're not talking

out of our asses in the heat of the moment?" Sal shot back.

"Everything that she already has in her own mind!" barked Ash. "Memories are subjective. We can't fuck with her perceptions and implant our own versions of things."

Sal shoved first, sending Ash stumbling back a few steps in surprise. "Get the fuck out of my face, fucking fairy wings."

"Say that again, little pussy."

Ash lunged for Sal, which seemed like a good time to step in.

"Hey, hey, hey now," I said, blocking Ash with my back while holding my arms out in front of Sal. "Looks like we could all use a little cooling off."

Sal's green eyes flashed with fury, but he turned and left the room with only a low growl. In the next moment, his presence was gone from the house. He probably left to set a chunk of forest on fire or whatever he did to let off steam.

Immediately, the tension decreased in the room. Ash let out a tired sigh and paced back toward the window. I knew he wasn't angry at Sal. At this point, we had grown used to his temper tantrums and always picking fights. At least this time, we knew it was out of caring for Deja.

Hell, both of their tantrums were for that very reason. It wasn't often that I was the calm in our storm.

"He has a point you know," I said after a few moments. "Deja feels like we're playing mind games and isn't happy about it. That could ruin everything."

"So what do you suggest?" Ash asked bitterly, leaning out over the windowsill.

I hesitated. He was not going to like what I had in mind.

"You should give her some space," I said. "Let me and Sal have some time with her, and we'll bring you back into her good graces."

"Heh," Ash scoffed. "You would suggest that. And what makes you think you won't make the same fuck up as I did?"

I walked up next to him and clapped him on the shoulder.

"We don't. That's just a risk we have to take."

8

DEJA

"It's called glamour," Diana explained. "Glamour is magic that tricks the eye into seeing something different than what is actually there."

"So that's how she disguised the covers of her books," I mused, blowing over the surface of my new chamomile tea blend.

"Exactly," she confirmed, picking up her own teacup. "You can apply a glamour spell to objects, buildings, even people and animals. Witch children often play pranks on each other by making slugs and such look like kittens."

"So it's easy enough for kids to do?" I asked hopefully. "And I can make it look like we're talking about something completely normal and not witchy?"

"Absolutely, dear. It's very simple to cast."

"What about the energy I felt through her palm against mine?"

Diana grinned. "She was revealing herself to you in the subtlest way possible."

"Hah!" I declared triumphantly. "I knew it was a secret handshake!"

My grandmother chuckled as she set her tea down and picked up her spell book.

"You said her aura had lots of greens and blues and was very shimmery?"

"Yeah, it was beautiful," I said. "It looked kind of like the Northern Lights, or how sunlight shines underwater."

Diana held one finger up in an *aha* motion as she flipped through the pages with her other hand.

"She is most likely a water witch, so it's no wonder you feel a need to connect with her," she said. "Earth and water are very supportive elements of each other."

"That makes sense," I mused, drinking my tea more deeply now that it was the perfect temperature.

My grandmother shot me an affectionate smile.

"I'm so glad to see you want to connect with another one of our kind, especially the same age as you. I was getting worried about you spending time with those--"

"I still haven't actually talked to her yet," I interrupted, unwilling to hear whatever she wanted to say about my guys. "She seems nice enough but who knows, we could end up being mortal enemies."

I still hadn't talked to Ash since last night, although I believed he was being truthful about the whole name thing. Still, just the sheer fact that he was purposely withholding information frustrated me to no end. I wasn't angry necessarily, just not in the mood to talk or definitely fuck.

After closing up shop, I made sure to hide the rose bouquet in the back room so Diana wouldn't see them when she came over. If she gave me shit for just hanging out with demons, I had zero intention of letting her know things were getting romantic.

"Well, that's always a possibility dear, but all signs point to you two hitting it off just swimmingly," Diana grinned. "Now shall we learn some glamour?"

The glamour lesson went smoothly enough. I got the hang of it after just a few practice casts. For fun, I disguised my mane of long, dark hair with a spiky blonde cut *a la* Miley Cyrus circa 2014.

"Interesting choice," Diana said with a chuckle.

"What, you don't like it?" I fluffed up the short pixie cut in the mirror. It even felt like real hair on my head.

"It's cute. I'm just not sure it's you," she mused. "All the women in our family had the most amazing dark hair." She brushed a hand through her silvery-white hair. "Well, until age caught up with us," she added with a dark laugh.

"I'll be honest. I could get addicted to this," I said, closing my eyes and focusing on the incantation as I drew another gesture in the air. When I opened my eyes again, my hair was now a pastel purple and fell in luxurious waves down to my waist, with my lip color matching my hair perfectly.

"I mean, this is seriously perfect magic for a night out," I said, twirling in the mirror. "Who needs an expensive trip to the salon when you're a witch?"

"For what is makeup and hair dye but another form of magic?" Diana said with a wink.

"You've got a point there," I said, running a finger along my lower lip. Not even a hint of a smudge. I wondered how badly Nona would freak out if I kept this look for work tomorrow.

"Well I'll get out of your long, purple hair for the night, dear," Diana said, gathering up her things. "Even though you look glamorous, I can see your eyelids drooping. Remember to get enough sleep while you're learning."

"I will," I said, holding back a yawn. Although

casting magic was always draining, I did notice my stamina improving. It no longer exhausted me like when I first started.

After a quick goodbye hug, I locked up the shop and headed upstairs to my apartment. My stomach let out a monstrous growl as I fumbled with unlocking the door. Damn, I skipped lunch and forgot to go grocery shopping. It would probably be takeout for dinner again.

If I weren't in the beginning stages of becoming *hangry*, the man lying comfortably on my couch would have been a more welcome sight.

"Sal!" I barked in surprise. "What are you doing in my house?"

He only lifted an eyebrow as a smirk spread across his face.

"What did you do to your hair?"

"Glamour," I muttered, my face reddening. "I was practicing."

While I enjoyed the pastel purple hair for the sheer fun of it, it would not have been my first choice if I wanted to make a guy's jaw drop. The look didn't exactly scream sexy bombshell.

"Looks nice," he said, lacing his hands behind his head while I tried not to stare. The position made his biceps look even bigger than normal. His legs and torso seem to stretch out for miles, making my poor little secondhand couch look as though it could barely support him.

"Really? Thanks. I mean, wait, nevermind." I let out a flustered breath. "You can't just hang out in my apartment when I'm not here. You guys need to have some boundaries."

He opened his mouth as if to protest but then quickly shut it. Instead, he abruptly swung his long legs off my couch and put them on the floor, resting his forearms on his knees.

"I'm sorry, Deja," he said with surprising tenderness. "I just didn't want to upset your grandmother." His serious face erupted into a naughty grin. "I'm sure you've noticed I can fly a bit off the handle sometimes."

"So can she when the topic of demons comes up," I muttered, settling on the couch next to him. "Avoiding her wrath is a valid excuse, I guess."

"The old lady gets under your skin," he said in a soft, observant tone.

"A little," I admitted. "She's a bit of a helicopter parent and doing it a bit too late. I mean, I met her not even a month ago and I'm almost thirty. I'm a little bit past the age of needing a mother figure in my life."

My hand dropped to Sal's knee. Why did it always seem to go there?

"I'm sorry, I shouldn't be complaining," I sighed. "I'm sure you didn't wait in my apartment to hear me vent."

"I'm here for whatever you need," he replied, skimming his fingers across my back. "And right now it seems you need to unwind."

His hand slid up to the nape of my neck and gently pinched the area between my neck and shoulder. My eyes rolled back and I let out an involuntary moan as his hands massaged the tension out of me.

"Close your eyes," he whispered, his breath tickling my ear.

"What are you scheming?" I asked but obliged.

"Now open your eyes," he said not five seconds later.

I did and my mouth fell open as well.

On my once-empty coffee table laid out a gorgeous assortment of food. Everything delicious and decadent imaginable seemed to take up the space. My eyes flitted over gorgeous red grapes, fancy-looking cheese, prosciutto, olives, dark chocolates, stuffed peppers, some cold noodle salad and so much more.

My stomach let out another approving growl, to Sal's amusement.

"Dig in," he said with a laugh. "I didn't know what kind of food you like so I whipped up a little of everything."

"Don't tell me you actually made all this?" I said, popping a cube of aged cheese in my mouth and letting the flavors soak into my taste buds.

"I did, although I conjured it. I didn't cook it."

I looked at him suspiciously as I chased the cheese cube with a tart grape.

"Very interesting skill set you have there, demon. War, violence, aggression, and... food?"

"Hey, we all need hobbies outside of our careers, right?" He slowly bit into a grape while staring at me and somehow just watching his jaw move hypnotized me. What kind of demon magic was he casting to make even chewing sexy?

Time seemed to slip away as we ate, bantered and flirted, but I was no longer tired. Either the food or his company, or a mixture of both, revitalized me with fresh vigor.

"I just realized something," I said after the fiftieth fancy cheese cube. "Where's your sidekick Raum? Hiding in my closet waiting to scare me?"

"No," he answered through more of his sexy chewing. "Just me tonight. I know you've been overwhelmed with everything and figured you wouldn't mind a more... intimate evening."

Heat spread throughout my cheeks as my stomach somersaulted.

"Not at all," I replied. "I really am glad it's just you."

As flattering as having three men's attention was, there was something about getting to know a person one-on-one that just couldn't be replicated with more people. Sal's undivided attention was also a welcome distraction to the awkwardness with Ash last night.

Despite eating my own weight in rich, decadent finger food, the table never seemed to run out and even a bottle of wine appeared out of nowhere. Sal wouldn't let me get up for glasses, so we passed the bottle back and forth.

"Oh God, I'm stuffed," I said, laying back with my hand on my belly.

At some point, my legs ended up in Sal's lap where he massaged my feet with toe-curling sensuality. His thumbs pressed into my arches, kneaded over the tender balls and heels of my feet with alternating pressure. I laid still, not wanting to shift even slightly and take away the bliss he was making me feel.

"Relaxed yet?" he asked, sliding his hands up to my ankles, inching just under my pant legs.

"Mm-hm. Mission accomplished."

My heartbeat quickened as he leaned over me, shifting his weight as gracefully as a cat. His thighs nudged my legs apart to straddle him as he placed his hands on either side of my body.

He brought his face dangerously close to mine. My body soared with heat and his green eyes flashed when he whispered, "Oh, I don't think my mission is accomplished quite yet."

9

DEJA

His low whispered statement directly contrasted with the kiss that followed. He brought his mouth crashing down on mine with a hunger that swept over me like an ocean wave, stealing my breath away.

That kiss was a match that engulfed me in fire. I clawed up his back to pull him down on top of me. When his hardness pressed into my center, I gasped so hard that I broke the kiss.

"Fuck me. Please," I moaned deliriously, already desperate for a release.

"I've been dying to," he rasped against my neck as he yanked my jeans down over my hips. "For so long."

When I peeled his T-shirt over his head, I had to pause and just look at him for a moment despite my animalistic needs.

"Holy shit, you're beautiful," I swallowed. "And I mean that in a totally masculine way," I stammered.

He merely chuckled as he finished removing my clothing and his, while I laid there entranced by how his muscles jumped and flexed as he moved. His skin was also dotted with scars, some of which looked downright lethal.

"What's this?"

I traced the lines of a tattoo on his ribcage, an upside down triangle with diagonal lines going through it.

"The sigil of Lucifer," he answered. "All three of us have one."

Another sigil was inked on his left side. I recognized it as the one he drew in the air that first night at the bar. But before I could ask about that one, he shoved his boxer briefs down his powerful thighs and successfully directed my attention *there*.

His cock bounced free, long and thick and pointing straight at me. My whole body throbbed with a powerful, needy ache.

"Now *you* are beautiful," he murmured, wrapping me in an embrace as he returned to laying on top of me. "And I mean that in a completely feminine way."

"Oh. Well, I'm relieved to hear that."

His laugh rumbled through his chest, vibrating against my skin. He felt so warm and solid and comforting. And he smelled amazing.

"Fuck Deja, I'm not even inside you yet and you feel incredible." He kissed the hollow of my throat before traveling lower to the valley between my breasts. "It's like I can feel you in my skin. In my bones."

"I feel the same way," I said, running my fingertips over the dark flames of his auburn hair.

It was true. This didn't feel like being with someone for the first time. It felt like a reunion after a painfully long time apart.

My skin sang with pleasure everywhere he touched me. Every kiss was a mouthful of fresh air. I felt like I was floating on clouds despite clinging to his hard, solid body. His mouth followed every curve and contour of me as if drawing a single line with his lips. But nothing was rushed about how he tasted and explored me. He took just as much time coaxing my nipples into diamond-hard points as he did kissing along my rib cage.

"Sal," I breathed, digging my nails into the hard landscape of his back. "You're killing me with all this teasing."

"And you're killing me with this body of yours. I need to take my time appreciating it."

He pressed another hard kiss to my mouth and a

sharp gasp escaped me when the firm, round head of his cock pressed against my sex.

I cinched my legs even tighter around his waist, locking my ankles together around his back and pressing every square inch of myself against him that I could.

He slid inside me in one fluid motion, tearing apart my softness with his hardness and filling the empty void within me.

"Fuck, Deja," he growled, skimming his teeth across my shoulder. "This is where I'm meant to be. Being inside you is home."

When he entered me, it felt like a key had unlocked something. I couldn't say exactly what, but a feeling of being open and free came over me. My past no longer defined me. It didn't matter. I had my magic and one of my lovers.

Every doubt, hesitation, and insecurity disappeared as Sal rolled his hips against me. My inhibitions melted into nothing as he filled me up with pleasure, stoking the flames of my desire into a roaring inferno.

A new desire soon filled me-- an overwhelming urge not to just lay back and enjoy, but to take control.

"Sit up for me," I moaned into his ear.

He obliged, wrapping one powerful arm around me as he leaned back against the sofa. His cock never left me but now I was in control. I secured my arms around his shoulders and soon found my rhythm riding his thick shaft.

"Mm, I love it when you're bossy," he groaned as he brought a hand between us to rub my clit.

He said that like we'd done this before. He touched me like he knew my body as well as I did.

Jolts of pleasure zapped up from my clit to my nipples, building up an intense pressure that threatened to burst.

I rode him harder, relishing in the sensation of him filling me up so deeply. He held my waist, guiding my thrusts with one hand while working my clit with the other.

My orgasm finally released and I convulsed around him. It was so much, so intense that I moved to lift myself off of his cock.

"No," Sal rasped, wrapping both arms around me and plunged back inside me to the hilt. "Let me feel you come."

He filled me up so impossibly much, toeing the line between pleasure and pain.

"Oh fuck," he groaned, holding me in place as he rocked against me. The friction sent smaller shockwaves through me, like miniature orgasms following the main event.

I slumped against him like all my bones had been liquefied. His pulse hammered underneath my ear with its odd-- but comforting--backward rhythm.

"Had enough already, beautiful?" he chuckled, smoothing his palms down my thighs.

"I'm a little spent," I admitted, feeling a bit bewildered. I never felt this tired after a single orgasm before. But then again I never rode a dick that hard nor came that hard before.

"No worries," he said softly, planting a kiss on my temple and coursing his fingers through my hair.

I lifted my head. "I never said that I was done with you."

He looked surprised and then pleased as I slid off his lap and knelt on the floor between his legs. I gazed at his heavy erection for a moment before stroking it, slowly rolling the velvety skin up the hard shaft.

"Ohh, fucking--"

His words stopped abruptly as I took him in my mouth, sealing my lips over his smooth head and pressing my tongue to the underside. As I worked into a steady pace, he breathed again, letting out wordless moans and sighs.

My mind reeled as I sucked and stroked him into a frenzy. I felt in control of my body, yet completely unlike myself. I had never been a fan of blowjobs in the past and definitely had no skill to speak of. But for some reason I was dying to taste him, to feel his hardness fill my mouth, and to hear his little gasps and moans as I pleasured him. It was making me wet again.

"Ohh yes, beautiful. Touch yourself."

I didn't even realize I brought a hand down to my clit until he said that. He became as hard as concrete in my fist and I knew he was close.

I moaned as I stuffed more of him down my throat, pressing my fingers in fast, hard circles on my clit for another release. I arched my back, putting on a dirty little show which drove him wild. I felt it by how his hips bucked as he fucked my face. His pleasure only made me hotter and I felt like a porn star.

He reached down to pinch my nipples and that was what set me off. My muffled moans of pleasure were soon followed by thick, salty bursts from his cock. I milked every drop from his balls and licked him clean.

He laid back panting on my couch as I rested my head on his thigh, grinning up at him.

"Had enough already, handsome?"

10

SALMAC

Deja's initial fatigue after her first orgasm didn't seem to last long. We went two more very satisfying rounds before collapsing into her bed. She drifted right off to sleep, breathing deeply and looking absolutely angelic in my arms.

I watched her while a feeling of peace washed over me-- unusual for a bearer of death and destruction.

Demons didn't sleep. At least we didn't need to like humans did, so I was content to hold her while watching her dream.

A tapping sound drew my attention to the window.

A large raven sat on the windowsill, tapping its beak on the windowsill and squawking, "Caw! Caw!"

My eyes shifted downward to Deja resting on my chest, my arms wrapped around her protectively. She didn't seem disturbed by the annoying bird's racket.

"Jealous, asshole?" I mouthed at Raum.

He tilted his head, watching us with beady black eyes before turning around and dropping a big bird shit on the windowsill.

"I'll let her know that was you."

Raum gave one more defiant tap to the window with his beak before flying away.

Deja stirred but didn't wake. Her eyes moved rapidly beneath her closed eyelids, signifying that she was actively dreaming. I wondered what she saw.

My hold on her tightened possessively as I recalled my near-fight with Ash, and I felt my white-hot anger returning.

He thought he knew what was best for her just because he was her first. But my connection with her was unique. She saw a side of me that no one else did, a side that I reserved only for her. And it seemed she instinctually picked up on it tonight. She jumped on me and rode me like I was a stallion only she could tame. Now if only she would remember our long, colorful history together.

Frustration grew within me like a buzzing wasp's nest. It felt like I was the only one who still yearned for her with all of my black, demonic soul, while the other two were content to wait even longer for her memories to return. Ash forbade us from even telling her how she forgot everything in the first place. And as impulsive and bullheaded as I was, he was my Lord and I had to obey.

But even a hothead like me could see his point. It would be unethical to color her memories with our own versions of events. She did seem to put a few more pieces together the more time she spent with us. Physical touch and intimacy seemed to speed that along, as that was the consistent bond between us, the connection that lasted even as she was reborn in different bodies throughout the ages.

"Mm."

She shifted in my arms, her eyelids fluttering slowly open this time.

"Good morning, sleeping beauty." Already I grew hard again just from feeling her skin move against me.

"Hm? Is it morning already?"

"Might be closer to afternoon now," I teased.

She lifted her head from my chest, gazing up at me with those feline amber eyes.

"You were Alexander the Great," she said matter-of-factly.

I couldn't hide my surprise, quickly followed by the joy blooming in my chest.

"So you're remembering more," I said.

"I am," she said, sitting up in bed and rubbing her

eyes. "I saw Ash before he fell too. Although there's still a big gap of time in between."

"But it is coming back to you and that's amazing," I breathed, unable to contain my relief. "Do you remember who you were when I was Alexander?"

"Roxana, his first wife," she said as if still in a daze.

"Yes," I confirmed, trailing my fingertips down her arms. "I went against the advice of all my generals and friends when I married you." I grazed my teeth against her ear. "And I'd do it all over again."

She flashed a wicked smile up at me. "Do you know what I did after you died?"

"No, what?"

"I killed those two bitches you married after me."

"I see my murderous influence may have rubbed off on you," I chuckled. "You know I married you out of love. The other two were for political reasons. It was normal at the time."

"I know. It's crazy how I just *know* that." She rubbed her temples. "It's like seeing a movie in my head but it's different because I was *there*. But that is so freaky to me because it was so long ago. I'm only twenty-eight years old for fuck's sake."

"It's a lot to take in," I agreed, pressing my lips to her forehead. "But it will get easier. And you'll remember even more."

She sighed as she curled up, snuggling into my

side. I could've spent eternity just holding her while she did that.

"How did I forget all of this information in the first place?" She traced the lines of my tattoos. "How could I forget all of you?"

I stiffened slightly, unsure of how much to tell her. The three of us didn't know if she remembered that event or if it had been wiped from her consciousness altogether. Not even Lucifer knew if she would ever recall it.

"Something happened," I said hesitantly. "A catastrophic event, at least for us. Someone deliberately set out to undo all the progress we made, that *you* made. They almost succeeded. It nearly broke all of us."

"Who's someone?" she asked in a small voice.

"The brainwashed angels who have not yet fallen," I said with more than a hint of bitterness. Ash spent centuries trying to recruit more of his winged brethren to our side, but the turnover was incredibly low. Fallen angels made up a small minority of Hell's residents. Most of them were created there, like me.

Deja let out a frustrated groan as she wrapped around me tighter.

"It still feels like we're speaking in riddles," she lamented. "I feel like I know half of what you're talking about and maybe-kinda-sorta understand some things but I'm still not getting it."

"You will," I promised, tilting her head up for a kiss. "And if we go another round, you might even learn more."

She grinned wickedly, throwing a leg over to straddle me. "You don't have to tell me twice, handsome devil."

I clicked my tongue and tapped my finger against her lips, shaking my head slowly.

Before she could respond, I lifted her up and flipped her over, laying her out on her back as my cock grew to full length between her legs.

I pinned her wrists next to her head and brought my face down to her neck while she squirmed in delight underneath me.

"This time I'm in control, beautiful," I murmured against her skin.

11

DEJA

I*s it possible to be hungover from sex?* I wondered as I stumbled into work the next day.

My body ached but deliciously so, like after a good workout. It felt more like the opposite of a hang-over, like nourishing my body with exactly what it needed.

I wondered if Sal felt the same way. He switched between being dominant and submissive at the drop of a hat and it constantly kept me on my toes. I never thought I'd enjoy a more dominant role in the bedroom but he drew that hidden side of me out like it was always there.

And maybe it was. Just for him.

"So uh, you got laid."

I spun around to see Nona giving me a knowing look.

"Is it that obvious?" I said.

"For not being a morning person, you have the most energy and pep in your step that I've ever seen. You're downright glowing. And on top of that, you have that smile and that look in your eye that says not only did you get it, you got it *good*."

"Yeah," I said casually, tucking a piece of hair behind my ear. "I guess I did."

"You guess? You're like a whole new person, Deja." Nona placed her hands on my shoulders and shook gently. "Who are you and what have you done with my boss?"

"Magical dick. What can I say?" I snickered. She had no idea how true those words were.

"Holy shit, call the news stations," Nona declared. "Deja said a male body part without blushing and nervously looking around."

I laughed but her observation was eerily accurate. I really did feel like a whole new person. From the moment Sal was inside me, a newfound confidence and boldness circulated through my veins. And it only grew each time we made love, along with the memories of my past lives.

Was this confident, uninhibited, sex-hungry woman who I really was? If so, I hoped this new Deja was here to stay. I was ready to shed my sheltered, repressed background like an old skin.

When Juno walked in the moment Nona turned on our OPEN sign, this new Deja brimmed with eager anticipation.

"Morning, Juno," I greeted jovially from the counter. "What can we get you this morning?"

"Morning! I'm feeling like a pot of Irish Breakfast, I think."

She pulled a few bills from her wallet but I waved her money away. "It's on me today."

"What? No." She blinked her wide ocean-colored eyes in disbelief. "Deja, I insist. This is my favorite tea shop, I want to support it."

"And I want to show my customers that I appreciate them." I pressed the bills she set down into her palm, sending a small pulse of magic through her skin as I did so. "You can support us next time," I added with a wink.

"Oh, that won't do. I'll just hand a fat tip to Nona when you're not looking," she said, a knowing smile spreading across her face.

"Feel free. Nona keeps her tips and deserves all of them." I prepared her tea tray and gently set it in her hands. "Enjoy your Irish Breakfast."

"Thank you, Deja. You really didn't have to do that," Juno said graciously before turning to find a place to sit.

As the morning rush came through, I hoped Juno would stick around until we had a chance to talk. I couldn't cast glamour with Nona so close by and hoped my secret witch handshake was enough of a signal.

By the time our pre-lunch lull gave us a moment to breathe, Juno's teapot was cold and empty. Still, she remained curled up and cozy in an armchair, looking completely at home.

I shoveled a sandwich in my mouth to hold me over for the next rush. When Nona took a bathroom break, I made my move.

My fingers danced through the air as I wrapped a glamour spell around Juno's armchair and the one right next to her. No customers even looked up as I crossed the threshold and took a seat across from her. To outsiders looking in, we were having a perfectly mundane conversation about tea.

"So you're a witch." I wasted no time the moment I sat down.

Juno looked up calmly from her book, an amused twinkle in her eye.

"I was starting to wonder if you would ever talk to me, witch-to-witch."

"This is all really new to me," I admitted. "I didn't know how or even *if* I should talk to you. I just learned glamour last night."

"Really?" She seemed surprised. "You wield your

magic so beautifully, with masterful skill. I was shocked I didn't already know you."

"Thank you," I said, feeling a blush rise in my cheeks for the first time that day. "It's a long story but I only just found out I was a witch not even a month ago."

"You're kidding!" Juno's mouth dropped open.

"No," I said and proceeded to tell her my life story, and how I came about knowing my truth. Or at least *one* of my truths.

I told her about growing up in the middle of nowhere, with my deeply religious parents and their community. How I never felt like I truly belonged but couldn't put my finger on why. My parents didn't approve of me going to college, for fear of my mind being poisoned with sin and worldly ideas. I got my first taste of the real world in college. I indulged in things like caffeine, alcohol, and premarital sex. I enjoyed the so-called sinful things much more than my strict, uptight home life, but guilt and obligation kept me from leaving home or pursuing a career.

It wasn't until last year that I cut the cord for good. I left home and took a Greyhound bus as far as I could afford, which happened to be San Francisco. I met Nona and started up my successful tea shop. Last month we went to a party and had our fortunes told by a tarot reader, who seemed to know an eerie amount about me.

Everything changed that night.

I started having dreams and Diana showed up at my place the next day. She informed me that my parents adopted me and I was born from a long line of witches.

"Wow." Juno's massive eyes stared at me unblinking. "That is one hell of a story."

"The exciting parts are, at least," I chuckled. "There's a whole lot of boring in between."

"If I may ask," Juno said gently. "What happened to your birth parents?"

"My mom died soon after I was born," I said truthfully. "And my dad apparently didn't want me so he took off."

I didn't want to get into potential death deals with demons, nor my current love life with said creatures. As nice as Juno seemed, she was still a stranger and I had no idea if she carried the same feelings toward demons as my grandmother did. Talking to another witch was great but my instinct was to protect my guys first.

"I'm so sorry," Juno said sympathetically. "I can't even imagine a childhood without magic, without that part of you being cultivated and encouraged."

The green tones in her aura shifted to a cool blue, indicating her empathy for everything I missed while growing up. I didn't feel pity from her though, which I appreciated.

"Well, I'm doing my best with the hand I was dealt," I replied.

Three hot men from the depths of Hell does make it a little easier in some ways, although they come with their own cans of worms.

"You are definitely catching up quickly! I never would have known," she said excitedly. "So is it just your grandmother teaching you? Do you have a coven?"

I shook my head. "You and she are the only two I know."

Except for the bartenders at Triple Moon, but no one else needs to see me necking in a dark corner with three demons.

"Oh, you've got to meet our High Priest and Priestess," Juno declared, leaning forward eagerly. "It can be hard to find a good community and they're very welcoming to newcomers. You could even attend a coven meeting and see what we're all about."

"Really?" I blurted, feeling like I was invited to a super secret, exclusive club.

"Yes, really. There's no commitment to join. They're actually very selective about who officially becomes coven members. You have to mesh well with the group and be dedicated throughout the long process. But there's no harm in casual meetings."

"A meet-and-greet doesn't sound bad," I said cautiously, although a tremor of nervousness fluttered in my stomach. Juno made no mention of the darkness in my aura yet, but Diana said it wasn't overwhelming. Would the older, more experienced witches be able to see it too and suspect demons in my company? And if so, how would they react?

"I'll give you my number," Juno said, pulling out her phone. "And we can arrange for you to meet Laurel and John, then take it from there."

"Sounds good," I agreed.

We exchanged information and only then did I look through the shimmery veneer of the glamour spell to check on Nona. The poor girl was dealing with a line going out the door, so I said a quick goodbye to Juno and jumped behind the counter to help her.

I mumbled my apologies as I flew back and forth, preparing orders with a renewed fire under my heels. The idea of meeting more powerful witches was both exhilarating and terrifying.

12

DEJA

As if I didn't have enough excitement for one day, Raum decided to show up right before closing.

"You guys will be the death of me," I said, my body already heating with desire.

His shoulder-length raven hair was tousled and slightly wet, like he just got out of the shower.

"Who says I'm here to see you? I came for the tea." His eyes lingered on me, indicating that was far from the truth. If I was still the old Deja, all his teasing might have actually wounded me.

"Take a to-go cup then," I ribbed back. "Give me less to clean up."

His teeth grazed his lips as they pulled back into a smile. He seemed pleased at my ability to take his teasing and dish it back.

"Only if you taste it first, to make sure it won't burn me." He leaned his muscular forearms on my counter, his dark eyes drawing me in like two black holes. "And leave a lipstick mark on the rim."

"You'd like that, wouldn't you."

My words wrangled in my throat. Already he was making me flustered.

"I'd like something else a lot more."

"I'm sure," I said in my best flirty but dismissive tone.

His eyes never left me as I did my best to ignore him while performing closing duties. I may have enjoyed it more than I should have. Leaning across the counter to give him a view of what he couldn't touch yet, bending over with my back turned to accentuate the length of my legs and curves of my ass.

He liked to play games, so I decided to play with him.

No sooner had I locked the door after Nona left did I feel him press up against my back, his solid chest like a hot, concrete wall against my shoulder blades and a rock hard erection against my ass.

"I'll make you sorry for that little show," he said gruffly into my ear, securing his arms around my waist and chest. "When I'm done with you, you'll be begging to cum. And if you're good, I just might let you."

Heat pooled in my center as his hands ravaged me, his rough stubble prickling the back of my neck and making my skin cry out for more.

In a stark contrast to Sal, Raum didn't appear to have a submissive bone in his body. He would claim me and my pleasure, punishing me for teasing him back. I would be at his mercy and I was dripping wet at just the thought of it.

"What's this about you shitting on my windowsill?" I asked, still wanting to defy him-- to see how far he would go.

"Hah. Sal's lucky I wasn't in human form." He pressed against me harder, pinning me to the door with barely any space to breathe.

"And who would have cleaned it up?" His presence was so overwhelming at that point, I was desperate to keep my head on straight.

"He would. You'd just have to order him to."

"And if I order you to let me go?"

His low, amused chuckle vibrated against my back, sending shivers across my limbs and directly into my brain.

"You'd be wasting your breath," he whispered hotly in my ear. "Because we both know you don't want that."

He attacked my neck with rough, biting kisses as his large hands kneaded my tender breasts through my shirt. Any words I had to dish back caught in my throat and turned to moans instead. My back arched as my hips pressed back, meeting him as he pressed forward.

"You want me inside you, ravaging you," he growled against my skin as he continued to man-handle me. "Bringing you to the edge again and again without ever letting you fall until I say so."

"Yes," I gasped.

He moaned his approval as his hands made their way to my ass, squeezing my flesh firmly as he rubbed his hot erection between my legs.

Clothing never felt so uncomfortable and restricting. I was burning up from his body heat pressing against me, plus my own pulsing fire building within me. But when his fingers slipped under the thin barrier of my top, I had to catch his wrist and stop him.

"Wait," I panted. "Let me turn around. Please."

His hard body pulled away from me slightly, just enough to spin and stare into his dark, lust-filled eyes.

"Something wrong?" he asked, his voice serious but strained with desire.

"No, I just--" I swallowed, my throat feeling like cotton as I willed myself not to get distracted by his eyes. Or his mouth. Or his arms flexing as they encircled my waist.

"I need to know something. I mean to ask whenever I see you guys but I kind of keep forgetting."

One side of his mouth ticked up into a smirk, indicating he knew exactly how distracting he and the others all were.

"I'm listening, gorgeous."

"I need a serious answer," I said sternly, meeting his gaze. "No riddles, no teasing. This is something important to me."

His smile dropped. His expression turned concerned as he brushed a light caress across my neck.

"Of course. Anything for you."

I took a deep breath, trying to quell the pounding in my heart.

"Do demons make deals with humans?"

He quirked an eyebrow. "You mean in the cliched 'selling your soul for fame and fortune' way?"

"Sort of," I said. "Or maybe killing someone and making it look like a certain cause of death? I'm not sure what kind of exchange that would be."

He remained silent for a moment before speaking.

"It's been known to happen," he said. "We have coexisted alongside humans for so long, some have made transactions like that. But it's incredibly rare."

"Why is that?"

His smirk returned.

"The moment a human wants to strike a deal with a demon, he already belongs to us."

13

RAUM

Deja's amber eyes sharpened as she took in what I said. Her breath still came out in little puffs from when I had her pressed against the door.

"Yes, I suppose that makes sense," she said absently.

Her expression flickered and I missed not a single detail. Something heavily weighed on her mind and compelled her to stop our intimate moment to ask this question.

"Why do you ask, little witch?" I traced a line along her sleek, feminine jaw. "Something else troubling you?"

She chewed her lip as she thought of an answer, and I wished it was my teeth instead of hers.

"My grandmother is convinced it was a demon's magic that killed my mother," she admitted. "She thinks my father made a deal with a demon because he couldn't handle having a child with a witch, and unmarried on top of that. But I keep thinking about it and it doesn't make sense to me. Why would a demon make a deal with a Christian to kill a witch?"

"Smart girl," I said, cupping her chin. "That's because it's absolute nonsense."

"It is?" Her eyes widened.

"Yes," I affirmed. "While it's true that witches and demons have a less than perfectly amicable history, we're often on the same side because the Christ-worshippers see us as all the same-- heathens."

"So it's not likely that a demon had a hand in killing my mother?" she asked. The hope in her voice was endearing and it made me pull her a little closer.

"It's possible, I suppose," I murmured into her forehead. "But yes, highly unlikely."

"But Diana said that was why my aura was so dark. I keep coming back to that and wondering why."

"I can tell you exactly why," I said, and she looked up at me expectantly. "It's because of who you are, and your long history with us. The history that you are slowly beginning to remember."

"Oh yeah. More of what you can't tell me," she sighed, leaning her head against my chest.

I pulled her hips tight against mine so she could feel how hard I still was.

"After I'm buried inside you, there won't be much more to tell." I kissed a slow trail down her neck to her shoulder. "You're already remembering, aren't you?"

"I remember you as both Odin and Loki," she breathed, her eyelids closing halfway as she melted into me.

"Yes, whatever the humans needed at the time," I affirmed, reaching down for her firm ass once again. "And you were?"

"A priestess of Freyja," she moaned, lifting one leg to wrap around my hip. "The goddess of love and fertility."

"And such a goddess you are," I growled as I pulled both of her legs up to wrap around me.

Instead of the wall, I opted to carry her to the counter, setting her down on the cool surface but still keeping my hands firmly attached to her ass.

"You used to turn invisible and fuck me in front of everyone at the rituals," she rasped against my ear. "They treated me like a queen because I had a direct line to the gods. They saw me being ravaged and possessed with their own eyes and fell to their knees saying your name."

"Mm, what good times we had," I groaned.

Her mouth found mine and drew the sweetest kiss from me. It peeled back all my barriers, released my resolve as I melted into her. I sought to dominate her mortal body but held my immortal soul between her lips.

She molded to my touch, leaning into my palms and pulling me closer eagerly. My sexy little witch seemed content with the answer to her question.

Still, I pulled back abruptly, leaving her breathless.

"Anything else you want to know?" I quipped.

"No. I'll let you know if I do," she said, reaching for me.

I grabbed her hands and placed slow, deliberate kisses on her wrists, watching her expression the whole time.

"Are you sure?"

"Raum, if you're not fucking me on this counter within two minutes, I'm kicking you out."

"Mm, sorry to disappoint, little witch." I drew in closer, pulling her thighs around my waist again. "It's going to take a lot longer than that."

I silenced her protests with a hard kiss, surging my tongue between her sweet lips until she caressed it with her own.

Her shirt came off first, in one swift movement over her head, and then mine. I released a groan as she trailed light, nibbling kisses from my throat and down my chest. She always used to do that and I loved it. Did she remember?

"It feels like I *know* you. Like we've done this before," she whispered. "It was the same with Sal. Logically, my brain is telling me this is the first time but I know how you are, and what you like."

"Because we *have* done this before," I told her, gliding my palms across her bare skin. "We know each other better than two human lovers ever could. You know that instinctually."

I captured her mouth in another deep kiss, relishing in her taste and the feel of her bare skin on mine. How good and right she felt after centuries apart was indescribable.

My fingers skimmed across her waist and belly to flick open the button on her jeans. I peeled her pants off her long legs, leaving her in a matching black bra and panties. She reached for my zipper but I pinned her wrists at her sides and grazed my teeth across her shoulder.

She wanted to tease *me?* Now the real teasing would begin.

Her panties were already soaked, and her mouth-watering, womanly scent filled my nostrils. I didn't dare touch her there with my hands yet, I'd be too tempted to let her cum too soon. Instead, I pressed my straining erection against her swollen, hot sex. One hand on her delicate waist kept her from squirming away as I sucked her shoulder and neck, my other hand inching under her bra.

"Oh, Raum," she moaned and gasped as I rolled her pert little nipples between my fingers. She clutched at my arms and shoulders as I continued mottling her perfect flesh, discarding her bra and sucking those sweet nipples between my teeth.

Her wetness began coating the front of my jeans from her desperate writhing against me.

"Ah, now look what you've done," I said in mock disappointment as I pulled away from her. "I can't go out like this." Her pupils dilated and her tongue lolled out hungrily as I finally unzipped and stepped out of my jeans. "How are you going to make this up to me?"

She dropped to her knees and rolled down my boxer briefs in a flash. Her eagerness to obey sent a heavy tightening in my balls. Fuck, she was just too perfect for me.

"Yes, that's my good little witch," I hissed, stroking her cheek as she glided her lips over my heavy shaft.

I wrapped her hair in my fist to hold her steady while I fucked her mouth at varying depths and speeds. Even when she had my cock in her mouth, I was always the one in charge.

She raked her hands down my thighs and moaned every time I stuffed her pretty mouth. Then she gasped for air every time I pulled out and held her tongue out for more. I thrust deeply into her mouth and pulled out for several minutes until I felt near bursting with cum.

"Because you sucked me so well," I said, sitting her back up on the counter. "I'll allow you one small orgasm."

"Thank you, Ra--ahh!"

My thumb pressed in slow, firm circles around her clit, still outside her panties. She panted and thrust against my hand, already on the edge of her release. Her perfect teardrop breasts bounced in my face and I couldn't contain myself from dipping my head and biting a nipple.

She came hard, screaming and thrashing against my hand. Her skin flushed a deep, beautiful red. I cupped her pussy and it burned against my palm like a warm stove.

My cock twitched and nestled against her thigh as I absorbed the heat from her body. She felt just like home. The moment it barely brushed her slick folds, she bucked and grabbed my hips to pull me closer.

"Please, I need you," she begged.

"Greedy girl," I scolded, but my chest tightened with pleasure at how badly she wanted me. She hadn't even recovered from her first orgasm yet.

I pulled her soaked panties aside and took half a step closer, resting my shaft on her clit hood. A deep, animal sound escaped me as I rocked my hips ever so slightly. Her hot bare flesh on mine was almost too much to bear. Even I couldn't handle the teasing much longer.

"Inside me, Raum," she whimpered. "Please fuck me."

"I'll fuck you when I'm damn well ready," I growled, but even my voice tremored as I began nearing the edge of my control.

She let out a shuddering sigh as I pressed two fingers inside her, working them at the same tempo as my cock caressed her clit. It wasn't enough, but my woman knew how to take what I gave her.

Her breath came in shorter pants as I felt her next orgasm building around my fingers. I curled them inside her as my heavy erection stroked her clit hood.

Every cell in my body was dying to sink into her as far as I could go, but I held back and watched her unravel for the second time. I felt her hammering pulse everywhere-- against my fingers inside her, in her lips as I kissed her, and it drove me wild like a blood-thirsty vampire.

She gazed at me hungrily with hooded eyes but knew better than to beg this time. Only good, patient girls got rewarded. And reward her I did.

Her breathing had barely slowed when I pushed inside her. I expected her scream, but not her third orgasm to release almost immediately around my cock.

"Fucking hell, Deja," I gasped, wrestling for control as I withdrew from her warmth and tightness. Despite teasing her into a frenzy and making this girl beg, she was the one really in control of me.

"I can't help it," she panted. "You feel too fucking good."

My impish grin couldn't hold back as I caught her mouth in another bruising kiss, sinking into her once again. I pushed her gently onto her back and pinned her wrists next to her head on the counter. Her eyes flashed with attitude but she didn't whine or beg.

Instead, her sweet pussy tightened around me as I rutted into her, relinquishing control to me and loving it. Her hips tilted up to draw me in deeper. Her sweet, submissive whimpers in my ear only drove me wild until I was slamming into her with all my might. She unleashed her final orgasm with a scream that echoed off the walls and finally ripped all my control from my limbs.

I collapsed and shuddered as I emptied into her, unrestrained pleasure sweeping across me. Her hands caressed me, bringing me back to earth from my high. Bringing me back home.

I caught her mouth in another kiss, but this one was different. Still passionate, but now an unspoken emotion passed between us. Something that could only be expressed with magic, not words.

And other demons wondered why I spent so much time in human form when I could fly as a raven. It was because nothing felt better than this.

14

DEJA

"Oh! There they are."

Juno stood and waved with a bright smile to someone behind me. I sucked down the last of my gin and tonic for a final dose of liquid courage, then turned to greet two of the most powerful witches in the city.

"Deja, this is Laurel and John. High Priestess and High Priest of the Golden Moon Coven," Juno introduced graciously, nodding her head in a slight bow.

"Oh please, no need for formalities," Laurel protested as she took my hand. "It's lovely to meet you, Deja."

"Juno has told us so much about you already," John

added, offering a warm, fatherly smile that immediately put me at ease.

"Good things, I hope." I settled back into my chair, nerves still fluttering in my stomach but not as bad as a minute ago.

John and Laurel were a fairly normal-looking middle-aged couple with salt and pepper hair. Laurel wore hers down her back in a long french braid that reminded me of Diana. They both dressed casually with a slight hippie vibe, complete with large chunks of raw crystals worn around their necks. John's aura was a pale, pastel green, while Laurel's was a shimmery, greyish silver. I sensed they were magical immediately but they looked so normal aside from that. I would never have taken them for witches.

"So did Juno show you this place immediately or send you on a wild goose chase?" Laurel asked in a teasing, motherly way.

I blinked, somewhat confused. We were sitting at Triple Moon Pub, the bar visible only to magical beings, which I happened to find the day after discovering I was a witch. And where I and three certain demons had done a fair amount of three-way making out.

I relayed this to Laurel and John-- save the demon part-- and they looked at me like I sprouted three extra heads.

"Hold on, let me understand this," John said, laying

a hand in the center of the table. "You learned you were a witch, started seeing people's auras, and just stumbled upon this place all within twenty-four hours?"

"More like twelve," I admitted. "I was about to go to bed the night before when my grandmother showed up."

He and Laurel exchanged a look that I couldn't read, but my stomach felt like it sank into my feet. I looked over at Juno, who had been silent since introducing us, and she merely lifted a shoulder in a half-shrug.

"Deja, who are your mother and grandmother?" asked Laurel. Her tone grew sharp and I suddenly felt as if I was being interrogated.

"Um, my grandmother is Diana Quinn. My mother's name was Deidre, but she died when I was an infant."

"I'm so sorry for your loss, dear." Laurel's sharp edge softened. "I know of your family of witches, albeit distantly. We're just baffled because, forgive me for saying this, but there is nothing special in your bloodline."

"Oh... kay." I wasn't sure whether to be offended or not.

"What Laurel means is," John cut in. "Your magic is highly advanced for being such a late bloomer, to the extent that it's usually a hereditary gift passed down through generations to be at your level of development. You've done in less than a day what typical witches can't do for years."

My mind spun and I began to regret drinking my alcohol so fast.

"Wait, so you're saying most witches can't see auras or find glamoured bars right away?"

"Places like this use a fairly complex glamour spell designed to keep underage witches from getting in trouble," John chuckled. "By the time they're of legal age, it can still be a few weeks before they see through it."

"Depends on how badly they want to drink," Laurell chimed in with a wink. "And yes, aura perception is a typically a learned skill that takes many years to hone, although some develop a talent for it while very young."

"Wow," I breathed, sitting back in my chair. "Diana told me I was learning fast but I had no idea."

"Told you that you were special," Juno teased, nudging me with her shoe.

"It's true," John agreed softly. "You are an exceptional rarity, miss Deja."

I didn't know how to feel. Flattered? Worried? Proud? More like a serious case of Imposter Syndrome. Just over a month ago, I was nobody special at all. Now I was apparently some kind of super-witch, as well as the reincarnation of some ancient still-yet-to-be-known person who captured the hearts of three powerful demons thousands of years ago.

Some inkling inside me told me these two pieces of information were related, although I couldn't be sure. And who could I possibly ask?

Laurel and John seemed nice enough but how much could I really trust them? My own grandmother's contempt for demonkind, not to mention the sideways looks I got from other patrons at the pub while with my guys, boiled my blood every single time. It felt like nothing more than blatant discrimination, just like being prejudiced against anyone else who wasn't them.

No, the only ones I trusted wholeheartedly were my demon boys.

Even Ash. Although my stubborn pride still wanted to be mad at him, deep down I knew he wasn't in the wrong. He wasn't trying to hurt me or jerk me around. He slipped up and then held steadfast to what he thought was best. I actually respected him for that.

Fuck. I missed him.

I hadn't seen him since that night I left his place. While the black roses he sent me never wilted, his aura around them began to fade.

Not that my time with Sal and Raum wasn't enjoyable. They each rocked my world in such special and different ways. But nothing could replace how my aloof, icy Ash melted like a popsicle when we touched. More memories of my past lives returned to me every night, but a large chunk of myself was still missing without him.

"It's a lot to take in, dear." Laurel's gentle voice cut into my thoughts, assuming my lack of talking was due to being overwhelmed with this new revelation.

"Um, yeah." I cleared my throat. "I don't really know what to say."

"You would greatly benefit from a supportive community, with mentors teaching you various aspects of magic that they specialize in," John said. "Your grandmother has clearly taught you well, but she is just one person. As your powers grow, you will need balance between them. And the best way to achieve that is to learn from multiple sources."

"But of course it's your decision," Laurel chimed in, shooting a sharp glance at John like a stern teacher. I began to realize that was her signature look. It seemed like she was the one truly in charge. "We absolutely don't want to pressure you, Deja. Lots of witches are solo practitioners because they can't find a coven that fits them, and that's fine too."

John mumbled something under his breath, indicating he disagreed with that last statement but didn't elaborate.

"I would like some time to think about it," I said cautiously.

"Of course, dear," Laurel said with a genuine smile. "We're having a gathering at our house on the next full moon. It's casual, so feel free to drop in or not. You'll be able to meet more coven members there. Bring your grandmother if you'd like."

"That sounds fun. I'll ask her," I said, feeling my defenses slowly back down. These people seemed good and honest. And my lonely heart did yearn for a community where I felt included. More than anything, I yearned for a *real* family.

"I'll be there, too," Juno piped up. "You can meet my boyfriend and other witches around our age." She rolled her eyes teasingly at Laurel and John, who both gasped in mock disbelief.

"Goodness, are you calling us old?" Laurel demanded, her hand flying to her throat. "If I wore pearls, I'd be clutching them right now."

We all laughed as a comforting warmth settled over me like a blanket. John went up to the bar to get us a round of drinks while Laurel asked me questions about my magic casting. I answered eagerly, the words spilling from my mouth like a waterfall.

And I thought maybe, just maybe, these could be my people.

15

DEJA

I opened my eyes to stare at a ceiling that seemed to stretch up for miles. The dark, oddly textured red walls converged but never seemed to meet. They just kept going up into infinite darkness.

Disoriented, I sat up abruptly and looked at my surroundings.

I realized I was not in my own futon at home but a massive, luxurious bed that also seemed to spread out around me endlessly.

The pillows and sheets were covered with a plush, silky red fabric, trimmed with an intricate gold pattern.

And a beautiful naked man laid across them next to me.

Ash's hair was longer, like the time I saw him as an angel before falling. His beard was gone and light stubble peppered his cheeks and chin. But his body was what took my breath away.

He looked like the statue of David come to life. Not a single flaw or imperfection could be found on him. His muscles were defined as if sculpted by the hand of an artist and in perfect proportion.

The beauty of him just made me want to cry. Sal and Raum were hot and muscular as well but still looked like relatively normal human men. One look at Ash and you just knew he wasn't created on Earth.

"Oh my God, Ash!" I gasped.

He laid on his back but I could see one of his wings peeking out from underneath him. What few white feathers remained were stained red with blood. The rest were charred or missing. And the angle of his wing seemed wrong, like the broken wing of a bird.

Only then did I notice the dark, tender bruises and welts on his side, wrapping around to his back. He looked as if he'd been burned, whipped, and pelted with rocks all at the same time.

But his eyes cracked open and he smiled at me like it was a typical, lazy Sunday morning.

"Hello, my love." His voice was gravelly with sleep as he reached for me.

"Ash, you're hurt!" I shrieked, too panicked to register his term of endearment.

"It's alright. Lucifer gave me something for the pain." He draped an arm across my waist and looked at me adoringly. "And with time, all will heal."

"But what happened?" I cried, hating that he'd been hurt so badly in the first place. I felt utterly helpless.

"We finally did it." He looked pleased, if a bit drugged out from whatever Lucifer gave him. "We rebelled. We took the fall. And I brought you with me."

"The fall?" I repeated as my mind scrambled to connect the dots.

"Yes, you're safe now." He reached for my hand and laced his fingers with mine. "No human man will ever make you submit to him again. You have all the same rights and powers as anyone else. All you have to do is take them."

As my thoughts raced, my eyes caught a mirror across from the bed and the reflection shocked me.

My eyes looked exactly the same golden-brown color. But other than that, I looked completely different. My hair was much longer, nearly down to my waist, and a shade of coppery auburn. With one glance down at my naked body, I saw I was much shorter and thinner. This was not the body I, Deja, was born in, and yet it was still mine.

"Lucifer suggests you form a legion to protect yourself," Ash continued in his lazy, sexy tone. "You won't be immortal like us but as the first human on our side, he will grant you powers over them." He eyed me curiously. "Or maybe he already has."

This had to be another one of my dream memories, right? There was no way I could wake up in a different body in a completely different place. But everything felt so real, from the sheets beneath me to Ash's arm wrapped around me.

And this raw power within me felt unmistakably real.

When I sat still and focused, I felt it traveling through me like millions of tiny high-speed trains. I closed my eyes and saw the Garden that was no longer my home. Yet still, wherever we were, I could draw the energy from the earth and will it to obey me.

"Turn over," I said abruptly. "Let me see your back."

Ash looked puzzled but obliged, rolling over on his stomach. I choked back a cry at what I saw. His injuries were far worse than I imagined. While the front of his torso was painfully beautiful and perfect, his back was a mess of deep gashes, mottled bruises, and painful welts. His left wing was a twisted deformity of broken bones with just a few feathers holding on. The right wing was gone completely, with a painful-looking, bloody hole where it once was.

If he were human, he simply would not have lived.

Steeling myself, I placed my palms carefully on his back and closed my eyes. I drew upon the resilient energy of the earth first up through my tailbone and collected it in the center of my chest. I had no idea what I was doing, and yet I did. It was pure instinct.

I drew on the healing powers of nature, which always returned with a vengeance even when the last little leaf fell from the tree. From the center of my chest, I willed the magic of the natural world through my arms and out my palms. I willed for it to heal my lover, my savior, like it healed the earth. To take away his pain, and to give him great black wings fit for a ruler of Hell.

I didn't open my eyes for the longest time, too afraid to see if I failed him. But when I saw my palms pressed against smooth, flawless skin and rippling muscles, I collapsed with relief and joy.

"It worked!" Tears sprang to my eyes as I smoothed my hands across his back, unable to believe it. "You're healed!"

Ash sat up and checked the mirror, looking over his shoulder with adorable fascination. He stretched his majestic black wings carefully and my breath felt stolen from my body. I never saw a creature that looked so beautiful.

"I'll be damned," he breathed.

"Well, considering we're in Hell, you already are," I giggled.

"No, my love."

With an impish grin, he folded them against his back again and dropped on top of me. An explosion of love and warmth spread from my chest as he pulled me into a tight embrace and peppered my face with kisses.

"I'm not damned in the slightest, even if I am a demon now." He shifted to look at me with his crystal blue gaze. "Because of you, my love, I am truly blessed."

16

DEJA

"Name your favorite flower off the top of your head," Juno instructed. "And go!"

"Any flower that's black," I replied. "I especially have a thing for black roses."

"Ooh, we've got a gothy witch," her boyfriend Erik teased.

"What can I say. It goes with everything."

I popped a cheese cube in my mouth, which was nowhere near as decadent as what Sal conjured up for me that night at my house.

My thighs clenched at the thought of my hot-tempered, yet sweetly submissive demon. I craved him like nothing else, except for Raum. And Ash, especially after that hyper-realistic dream of healing his back and giving him new wings.

That still shook me hard. I couldn't get it out of my mind. It felt so real, it *had* to have really happened.

I looked across the room to where Diana, Laurel, John, and a few older witches gathered, talking in low voices. They sat around a small coffee table with candles, crystals, and herbs arranged in front of them. On the way here, my grandmother had kept her anti-demon rhetoric to a minimum, thankfully. But coming to this party with her reminded me of what Raum told me. Demons didn't bother making deals with humans, especially not against witches.

It led me to wonder how she came to the conclusion that it was demon magic that killed my mother. Despite admitting she had no proof, my hope lingered that she based her theory on some actual evidence, maybe some ancient ritual or pact, not just prejudice.

Juno, Erik and I hung out in the kitchen with a few other coven members who looked to be in their twenties and thirties. From the moment Diana and I walked in, I gravitated toward Juno's clique and Diana immediately started catching up with Laurel and John. Apparently, they were part of neighboring covens back in the day.

Across the kitchen island from us stood a guy introduced as Seth, drinking a beer and mainly keeping to himself. But I felt his eyes on me like an itch on my skin that wouldn't go away.

I did my best to ignore his gaze. With his tousled dark hair, stormy gray eyes, motorcycle jacket, and tattoos peeking out of his shirt, it was difficult. His bad boy image reminded me of my guys and even friendly eye contact sent a nervous fluttering in my center. If I didn't know any better, I'd suspect he was a demon in disguise. Even his aura was nearly as dark and electrically charged as theirs.

"Care for a smoke?"

Erik tapped a pack against his palm as his eyes flickered across all of us. Juno and I declined but Seth gave a curt nod. The guys headed for the backyard and with Seth gone, the intensity instantly fizzled out of the room.

"Are you having fun?" Juno asked, giving me a playful poke on the arm.

"I am," I admitted with a smile. Laurel and John's home was just as comforting as their presence at the bar. They were incredibly hospitable hosts and the coven members I met seemed warm and welcoming as well. It truly felt like I was among friends.

"I think Seth likes you," she teased.

"Really? 'Cause I get the impression he'd enjoy carving my eyeballs out with a spoon."

Juno laughed. "He's just really intense. He actually

hasn't been around much in the last year. He's been traveling to all kinds of places like Iceland, Romania, and I think Africa, too."

"Oh yeah, doing what?"

"Hunting demons," she remarked casually.

17

DEJA

My blood turned to ice. I tried to keep my expression blank while my heart stopped in my chest.

"Oh, really. That's a thing, huh?" Keeping my voice steady felt impossible but Juno didn't seem to notice.

"Yeah, I don't know much about it," she remarked, dipping a celery stick into ranch dressing. "Just that it's incredibly dangerous and very few witches take on that role. It's kind of an elite, secret agent thing."

"Hmm," I mused, sipping my beer and trying to keep calm. But my insides swirled with panic. What kind of abilities did he have? Could he tell just by looking at me that I kept company with the same creatures he hunted?

The guys returned from smoking before I could properly settle down. And Seth's intense gaze now only made me want to run off and warn my guys as soon as possible.

"Deja, right?"

Naturally, that was the time he chose to unmute himself.

The scent of cloves and woodsy cologne hung around him like a cloud as he popped a mint into his mouth.

"Yeah." I forced a tight smile.

"It's a sexy name." His mouth twitched into a smirk, daring me to tell him off.

"Uh, thanks." *Please don't ask if my last name is Vu.*

"You know what it means, right?"

"Remembrance," I answered tersely. "In the age of Google, is there anyone who doesn't know the meaning of their name?"

"Little spitfire," he drawled. "You sure you're an earth witch?"

"Scorched earth, maybe," I sneered, setting my drink down. "Now if you'll excuse me, I must be going."

"Leaving already?" Juno asked with a frown.

"Yeah, sorry," I said, pulling her into a hug. "I have an early morning at the shop tomorrow."

I said my goodbyes to everyone else, including Diana after confirming she'd have a way home, and stepped out into the chilly night air.

A single raven cawed from where it sat on a telephone pole, then took flight in the direction of my apartment.

"Wouldn't mind having that power myself," I muttered, hurrying down the street to the train station.

My leg bounced with anxiety the moment I sat down. It was only a ten-minute ride but seemed to take an eternity before I reached my stop. When I was finally walking again, my legs couldn't seem to move fast enough.

I finally burst through the door of my apartment to find Sal and Raum sitting on my couch. It didn't even bother me that they waited in my house anymore. I was getting used to it, and maybe even found it comforting. But under these circumstances, all I could feel was panic.

"Where's Ash?" I demanded, breathless. "I need all three of you here."

Sal approached me first, his face a calm exterior over the fire within.

"He still wants to give you space, beautiful. Until you remember your original name."

"What the fuck?" I cried, exasperated and my heart aching for him. "I'm over the name thing, okay? This is important. I need to see him."

"He knows you're not angry," Raum said from the couch. "It's not you. It's just that he doesn't trust himself to keep it from you."

I speared my fingers through my hair and let out a frustrated groan. Didn't he know how much I missed him? How could he keep avoiding me like this? This was life or death and he was hung up on my stupid memories.

"What's wrong, beautiful?" Sal grabbed my waist and tugged me forward. His lip curled into a threatening snarl and I could already feel his rage rising.

"There's a demon hunter here," I said. "His name is Seth. He's part of the local coven."

Sal cocked an eyebrow. "No one I've ever heard of."

"I have. He's nobody," Raum said in a bored tone.

"What do you mean?" I demanded. "He hunts demons!"

"He destroys the bodies of lower demons, which doesn't actually kill them," Raum explained. "Their souls are sent back to Hell, where they wait to inhabit another body."

"Are you sure?" I asked skeptically. "My friend said hunters are elite witches and have dangerous jobs."

"'Cause they're so incompetent, they get killed more often than they actually kill." Sal scoffed, tightening his hold on me and bringing his mouth close to my ear. "Trust me, beautiful. He's no match for the likes of us." Abruptly he pulled away just enough to look at me.

"But if he gives you any trouble, make no mistake. We'll hang him by his scrotum."

I snorted a laugh but couldn't fight the heat pooling in my body. I leaned into his chest, his strength. It absolutely killed me how he could be so sweet and so vicious.

"Other than that, how was the witch party?" Raum asked, his clever grin widening.

"Other than that, Mrs. Lincoln, how was the play?" I mocked. "I'm glad you two are so nonchalant, but I had to keep my cool while talking to someone who I thought was going to *kill* you guys! I could've had a heart attack on my way up here!"

Sal made a growling noise into my neck and all my frustration seemed to melt away.

"It's so hot that you're protective of us," he murmured. "And we'd do the same for you, beautiful."

He led me to the couch, seating me between him and Raum. His firm hold moved up to my back, where he rubbed the tension out of my shoulders while placing light kisses on my neck.

My head leaned back as my back arched, melting into his touch. In front of me, Raum slid his hands up my thighs and pressed his lips to my exposed throat.

"Neither one of us is Ash and I know that you miss him," he murmured. "But maybe the two of us can help put your mind at ease?"

"At the same time?" I gasped, more thrilled than shocked. Thoughts of a threesome no longer made me want to blush and hide, but I had yet to experience any true memories of it. This would truly be my first time.

"If that's what you want, beautiful," Sal murmured against my nape.

I reached behind me to feel across his lap. He was already hard and growing bigger. The hollow ache inside me grew as he groaned and muttered curses under his breath.

I kissed him over my shoulder as I stretched my other hand forward, skimming my fingers up Raum's thigh as he did to me. When I found him growing hard too, a deep gasp of pleasure escaped me and left me breathless.

"Seems like that's a yes," he chuckled, dipping his head lower to kiss down my sternum.

Sal's tongue surged into my mouth with renewed hunger as he continued his massage under my blouse. He peeled it over my head while Raum pulled my leggings down over my hips. Their shirts disappeared too and while sandwiched between them, all the bare skin contact put me in absolute heaven.

Sal's heart thundered against my back while he sent light caresses over my arms and shoulders. Raum grabbed my hips and forcefully tilted them up as his kisses grew dangerously close to my pussy.

Already I quivered in anticipation. Two pairs of hands on me and the gorgeous men attached to them were almost too much to bear.

I leaned against Sal like he was a solid wall. Raum's back and shoulders flexed before me as he wrapped his large hands around my thighs. He drew teasing circles around my vulva with his tongue, making me shudder and press my hips up higher to meet his mouth.

The two of them were so in sync, it felt like they shared a single mind. Sal's gentle touches and kisses on my neck contrasted sharply with Raum's rough handling and merciless teasing.

When Raum finally sealed his mouth over my pussy, Sal cupped my breasts and held me in place. His thumbs soothed the sensitive ache in my nipples while I helplessly tried to thrash against Raum's mouth. He ate me out roughly, greedily. The friction of his stubble sent my hot, sensitive skin into overdrive. I couldn't pull away to ease back on the sensation, it was too much all at once.

My first orgasm exploded within a minute, leaving me stunned and gasping. I barely felt it build up at all.

Raum grinned wickedly up at me as he kissed each of my trembling inner thighs.

"Why don't we switch, brother?"

"Excellent idea," Sal's voice rumbled behind me.

The hard wall of his chest disappeared behind me

as the guys traded places. Seconds later, Raum's different but no less solid form took Sal's place.

"Let's get you nice and spread for Sal, my good little witch," he growled into my ear as he took each of my thighs in his strong grip and pulled my legs apart.

I was spread out and exposed, already panting and covered in a thin sheen of sweat, and Sal looked at me like he wanted to drop to his knees and worship my body.

His touch was firm but gentle. His smooth face and tongue soothed my roughened skin. He licked and kissed me tenderly where Raum had been so rough just seconds before. I could still feel the friction of his stubble and Sal's softness on top of that drove me wild. They were a perfect balance, like two opposing forces of nature that both felt so fucking good.

"How does his mouth feel, my sexy little witch?" Raum demanded, his low, rumbling voice sending goosebumps along my neck. "Is he getting you nice and wet for the fucking you're going to get from me?"

"Yes," I moaned deliriously. "It's so good."

Sal hummed with pleasure as he pressed two fingers inside me, stroking my inner walls while his tongue tirelessly caressed my clit. Heat and an aching need to release began building up within me. I reached down and threaded my fingers through his fiery auburn hair until Raum pinned my arms back.

"No cheating," he scolded with a grinning bite to my shoulder. "Let him get you off at his pace."

I whimpered and whined as Sal slowly walked me to the very edge. Raum scolded and punished me every time I fought for control. He pinched my nipples, bit hard on my neck, and told me exactly how hard he was going to fuck me when Sal was done.

I finally came so hard that magic sparked from my fingertips. Convulsions and pure, blinding pleasure wracked me. I completely lost control of my body.

At that point, all three of us were fucking done with the foreplay. My men continued with their opposing gentle and rough forces and it was nothing short of magical. Raum fucked me hard from behind and made a mottled, bruised mess of my ass while I stroked Sal to the edge of his own orgasm. Sal flipped me onto my back and made love to me with such intense passion while Raum rammed his cock down my throat. I swallowed his massive load and licked him clean while Sal emptied himself inside me.

I felt filthy and used, empowered and worshipped, loved and cared for all at the same time. A good cathartic cry didn't even come close how emotionally intense the experience was. I realized I *needed* Raum's dirty talk and rough handling just as much as Sal's warmth and sweetness.

They carried me to bed when we finished and

wrapped around me with kisses, caresses, and good nights. As my exhausted but sated mind drifted off to sleep, it made me wonder how anyone could be satisfied with just one person.

18

DEJA

A sensual mouth left a burning hot trail of kisses down my back. Rough stubble grazed over my skin, making me shiver.

A second pair of lips kissed my forehead while fingertips skimmed down my bare thighs.

Still mostly asleep, I shifted my weight and found my cheek pressed against a warm, hard chest. The watery backward heartbeat quickened under my ear.

These were the dreams I both loved and hated. Such vivid and hot sensations in my body, but I could never see who was with me. Every time I opened my eyes, I only saw darkness. Like I was in a dark room and my lovers were invisible.

My body yearned for their touches every night. I hated the moment I woke up, the moment they disappeared.

But this time my eyes cracked open to find a pair of green ones staring back at me.

"Good morning, beautiful," Sal greeted, sliding his hand down my thigh to gently knead at my calf.

Behind me, Raum's trail of kisses down my back turned toward my hip bone, where he playfully bit me.

"Good morning, my handsome devils," I croaked, stretching out between them. "So last night was real, huh?"

"As real as we are here in your bed." Raum rested his head on my thigh as I snuggled back into Sal's shoulder. Being sandwiched between them filled me with the utmost contentedness and warmth.

"How are the three of us able to fit in here?" I lifted my head to see the guys had plenty of room on each side of the bed. Considering their large, muscular frames on my full-sized futon, that seemed impossible.

"Magic," Raum smirked, although he wasn't joking. "Hey, I don't mean to alarm you," he murmured lazily, resting his cheek against my hip. "But your phone has been blowing up."

"Huh." I frowned. That literally never happened. The shop was closed today and there would be no other reason for anyone to call me nonstop.

"You asshole," Sal groaned, pulling me back into his

chest as I started to get up. "Now you're making her want to get out of bed."

"Well, you keep hogging her over there," Raum replied. "As much as I love this backside," he declared with a slap to my ass. "You're stealing all the snuggles and the kisses."

"Aw, what's that?" I flipped over to face him, my grin spreading the moment I saw his pout. "Mr. Dirty Talk and Dominant wants cuddles and kisses?"

"I'm grumpy without my sugar in the morning," he growled before cupping my chin and lowering his mouth to mine.

His slow, sensual kisses turned me to jelly. My brain shot off fireworks as it reconciled this was the same man who made me choke on his cock last night.

Our tongues spoke their own language as they caressed and danced. He told me without words how much he cared about me, and that he would never hurt me unless I derived pleasure from it. I folded my arms against his chest and he cradled my back as gently as if I were a baby.

Only when I was completely lost in the taste and warmth of him, did his kisses grow deeper, more demanding. Hot moans escaped from deep in his chest as his grip on me tightened. The demon couldn't hold back for long.

He palmed each of my breasts and grazed his teeth down my neck. I slid my hand down the ridges of his abs and stroked his thickening length, growing harder by the second.

Another hard cock pressed against my slick vulva and I let out a gasp of surprise. Sal grinned wickedly and gave me a kiss over my shoulder as he rubbed against me.

"It's pretty hot watching you two, so I'll enjoy this beautiful backside for now."

With a firm hand on my hip, he stroked himself against my swollen pussy while I stroked Raum.

"Oh, that's so good," he moaned, halfway closing his eyes. "My sweet little witch."

He twitched, moaned, bit his lip, and even yelped a little as I glided his smooth skin up and down. Watching my dominant one, the trickster, the tease, the one always a step ahead, lose control in the palm of my hand was unbelievably hot.

"Ahhh," I cried out in both relief and ecstasy as Sal finally slipped inside me. He pumped into me steadily, my pussy already slick from him teasing me so much.

Raum sealed his mouth over mine as his fingers found my clit. He grew as stiff as concrete in my hand. I stroked him faster. We swallowed each other's moans as our pleasure soared to new heights before crashing all around us.

I shattered around Sal's cock and he let out a string of curses, reaching around to grab my breast and fucked me deeply before releasing inside of me.

Raum's breath grew ragged as I continued to stroke him. He looked somewhere between tortured and drunk, but still insanely sexy.

"Your mouth," he rasped right before the end.

I slid down the bed and brought him to my lips just in time. He let out an animalistic growl and his whole body stiffened as his cock convulsed, coating my tongue in thick, hot cum.

After swallowing my fill of him, I slid back up to snuggle against his chest this time, letting Sal spoon me from behind and kiss my shoulders. Such deep relaxation settled back into my body.

"How's that for your morning sugar?" I murmured against Raum's hot skin.

"Mmm. The best I've ever had, baby," he whispered as he wrapped around me tighter.

All the skin-to-skin contact made me feel incredibly cozy and protected. I nearly drifted off to sleep again before I remembered.

"Oh yeah," I said, sitting up. "My phone."

19

DEJA

"Call me as soon as you can. I need to talk to you about something important."

Juno's message glared up at me from my screen. It was the only text she sent among a slew of missed phone calls.

I hurriedly called her back, panic rising in my chest as the worst-case scenarios ran through my head.

"Hello?" she chirped in her usual cheerful tone.

"Hey, what's going on?" I demanded. "Is everything okay?"

"Yeah, everything's fine," she laughed. "Did I worry you?"

"Um, yes. What is so important that you need to call me at least fifteen times?"

"Nothing bad, trust me," she said. "But I thought you should know I overheard Laurel and John talking to your grandmother last night after you left."

"Oh? About what?"

Sal chose to walk by just then, completely naked and whistling cheerily. He winked at me as he headed toward my kitchen. My heartstrings pulled tight as I watched the perfect globes of his ass flex before my eyes. What I would kill to make sure I had that view every single morning.

"It sounded like they want to initiate you into the coven really early. Normally it takes one year and one day for a new witch to be initiated. But your grandmother was talking about your powers and how fast you learned. Sounds like they might make an exception for you."

"Wow, really?"

Excitement lifted my heart for a fleeting moment before I remembered Seth's sullen face and stormy gray eyes. Could I really stand to be around a demon hunter, even if he wasn't a threat to my guys? Even if his power didn't hold a candle to them, something about him rubbed me the wrong way.

Not to mention everyone else in the coven. If they accepted and supported a demon hunter among them, how would they feel about someone who slept with the ones he hunted?

"I don't know, June," I said, running a hand through my sexed up bed hair. "It's still a lot to take in right now.

"I totally understand," she said. "Talk to your grand-mother about it, see what she says. But I gotta say, it would be so cool to have you officially with us. We would be sisters!"

Something pulled at me when she said that and refused to let go. I never had a sister before. Hell, I never felt like I had a real family until recently.

A sudden kiss on my cheek startled me out of my thoughts.

"Let's see what kind of tea you have stashed here," Raum smirked as he, also completely naked, joined Sal in the kitchen.

Both of their perfect, biteable asses hovered in my view as they raided my cupboards. My heart ached with the sensation of being pulled in two opposing directions. I wanted a witch family more than anything, but I would never let go of my demon lovers. They were mine for eternity.

"Unfortunately Seth won't be around much to make googly eyes at you," Juno teased, cutting into my thoughts. "But I could introduce you to more magical guys if you want."

"Oh, hm?" I said, feigning interest as if three men

weren't enough to handle. "Seth's off on his uh, business?"

"Yeah, sounds like he's leaving for the Amazon jungle or somewhere tomorrow. Lots of evil spirit activity."

"I see." Joining the coven without him around sounded much more appealing, though I still had my doubts.

"You still there?" Juno asked gently.

"Yeah, sorry." I blew out an exhale. "Just a lot on my mind. I'll call you later with a more definitive answer."

I ended the call and strode into the kitchen to join my two naked men. Sal held out a steaming mug of Irish Breakfast to me.

"I don't have your skills but I think the caffeine will do the job," he said with a sheepish grin.

I took a tentative sip. "It's perfect," I said, standing on tiptoes to kiss him. "Thank you, my lion." The nickname tumbled out automatically like muscle memory, even though I never knowingly called him that before.

Sal looked just as surprised as I was, but with more joy and less confusion.

"You're remembering," he said, his voice thick with emotion. "That's what you always used to call me."

"The body of a warrior and the head of a roaring lion. A god of war. The creator and destroyer of cities." My mouth moved as if controlled by someone else, but the images came to me as clearly as if I'd been there.

Because I *had* been there.

Like it was yesterday I saw myself walking next to Sal on an ancient, bloody battlefield, his lion head roaring victoriously. I saw him the moment he was created in that cavernous throne room in Hell. He dropped to his knees and pledged his undying loyalty to me.

"Yes," I breathed. "I'm remembering so much of our time together now." Tears welled up in my eyes as seven thousand years of love and adoration for this man hit me all at once. His passion fueled his fury. And the unique connection we had was the only thing that tempered his flames.

"And you, Raum." I turned to my dark-eyed demon to find a rare, serious look on his face. "Your visions used to hurt you. They would come on suddenly like violent headaches that you couldn't control. Nothing I did could take the pain away. I would just hold your head in my lap until the vision faded."

"Just your hands on me helped with the pain a little," he replied. "You were my immediate pain relief. But I learned to control it, after a few centuries."

I leaned into him while reaching behind me for Sal's hand at the same time. Surrounded by warmth and affection on all sides and my heart stilled ached for Ash. I missed him terribly, now that I could feel the full weight of being without these men for so many lifetimes.

"What do you two think I should do?" I said after a long silence. "Join a coven where they accept people who hunt your kind? Or tell them to fuck off and strike it out on my own?"

Raum's chuckle rumbled against my chest. "You wouldn't have kept us around so long if we were the kind that told you what to do."

"Even if we did, it would ensure you did the exact opposite," Sal agreed.

"I just hate that those who've opened up to me, accepted me, and want me to grow, are the same people who want me to stay away from you," I groaned.

"That's the way the cookie crumbles sometimes." Sal took a sip from my Irish Breakfast while I openly stared at him in bewilderment. How could he of all people feel so nonchalant about this?

"This situation has happened several times before," Raum said, noticing my confusion. "Think of yourself as an undercover agent. Infiltrate the enemy, befriend them. And slowly make them see the error of their ways."

"Can you see the outcome?" I asked, looking up at him. "Will I be able to make them come around to you guys?"

"I have seen it," he confirmed. "But whether good or bad, I can't change what's already set in motion, nor can I use my sight to influence your decision making." His playful smirk dropped once again. "The last time I tried desperately to change an outcome, we lost you anyway."

I draped my arms around his neck and he nestled his large hands in the curves of my waist.

"If we've learned one thing," he murmured against my forehead. "It's that existence as a whole is much bigger than us. What happens in one year, one lifetime or even one century is just a small building block in the grand scheme of existence. We've been trying to steer the course for millennia. Sometimes we make great strides, other times we're pushed back." His smile returned. "As long as there's a need for a little corruption, our work is never done."

"So you're saying it doesn't matter in the big picture if I join this coven or not," I said. "I'll still have lifetimes to master my magic and steer the course of history with you three."

"Exactly." Sal brushed a kiss along the nape of my neck. "We know your loyalty is with us. Just as we are eternally loyal to you."

"Always," I said, turning and locking my gaze on his emerald eyes. "My instinct is always to defend and protect you three. Now that I know why, I swear I won't let any of them hunt you."

"We're not concerned about you leading them onto us, beautiful," he said with a fiery spark in his eye. "Infiltrating the enemy is what you do best."

20

DEJA

I shed my clothing under the silvery moonlight and waded slowly into the stream.

"Wow, you're brave," Juno remarked. "It's freezing out here."

"Just gotta jump in and do it," I said.

The goosebumps erecting along the entire length of my body agreed with her, but while my skin was cold, my core roared with heat like a furnace. The slippery rocks and mud between my toes acted like heat sources. Already, I was calling on the magic of the earth to guide and strengthen me through the initiation rite.

Juno waded in after me once I found a comfortable

spot to sit. She remained dressed in her ceremonial black and gold robes as she helped me bathe. The untouched, natural spring water ran over my arms, back, and hair with her assistance. When every bit of my skin and hair had been kissed by the freezing water, we stepped out and she dried me off with a towel.

We huddled by our fire for warmth as she brushed out my hair. I opened my bag and carefully unfolded the long, white robe I would be wearing in the ceremony. I pulled it over my head while she adjusted and secured it in place.

The hardest part for me was done. Now just came waiting.

I sat cross-legged in front of the fire as Juno mixed a concoction with her mortar and pestle. The flames danced and flickered as it fed on the dry branches. Beneath me and all around me, earth magic hummed with energy. Even a single dry leaf on the ground made my toe pulse with its life force.

No other form of magic felt like a better fit for me. Nature was constantly in flux but always in perfect balance. Death gave birth to new life. Earth contained the power to heal as well as destroy.

"Close your eyes," Juno instructed.

I obeyed and felt something cool and wet on my forehead as she painted with her fingertip. She drew the symbol of earth on my forehead and continued with more symbols on my cheeks and chin with the concoction she mixed.

Coven tradition dictated that I choose the concoction but another member mix and apply it. I chose ash from the fire, mud from the stream, and wild juniper berries that grew native to here. All unique components of the single element of earth.

"I'll come for you when they're ready," she said once she was finished.

I nodded while keeping my eyes closed. The mixture felt refreshing on my skin and my face pulsed everywhere it touched.

Laurel would be leading the rite as High Priestess. She and the other coven members were gathered in a clearing in another area of the woods. Before I could join them, I had to be washed and painted, then they had to purify the ceremonial circle.

I sat as still as a boulder, feeling the earth's magic flow through me as if I were an empty vessel. I imagined it as a thread starting from my tailbone rooted to the ground, then flowing out through the crown of my head to return to the universe.

The crickets chirping and burning logs snapping sounded like music to my ears. Tears threatened to well up just because of how beautiful and moving it all was.

Then like a gust of wind, the energy shifted

dramatically and I knew I was no longer alone by my fire.

"Ash," I said in a choked whisper. He may not have been there physically but I felt his aura wrapping around me like a strong hug. My heart physically ached for him. I missed him so much.

"My love," came his voice, sounding like he was speaking directly to my brain. "When will you remember the woman I fell in love with? I miss her with all of my being."

"I miss you too," I cried out. "I'm right here."

The magic coursing through me took another sudden shift, this time leaving me breathless and gasping. My eyes flew open as I lurched forward, catching myself before diving headfirst into the fire.

I struggled to catch my breath as my heart crashed like a sledgehammer against my ribs.

I remembered now.

I knew exactly who I was.

A fiery sigil hovered above the flames, the same one Sal drew when I first drank with the three of them at Triple Moon. The one tattooed on the left side of his body, the side of his heart. I now knew it was *my* sigil and traced it with my fingers.

I said my name out loud, the first name I was ever given, and Ash's aura wrapped tightly around me again.

"Finish your rite, my love," he whispered. "I'll see you after it's done."

My breathing calmed just as a large snake slithered across my lap, its forked tongue tasting the air. I smiled and patted it affectionately.

"Thank you, Lord Lucifer, for helping me return to myself as well as my three eternal lovers, my Unholy Trinity."

Branches snapped as a ghostly figure in a long white robe approached me from the treeline.

"They're ready," Juno said with a wide grin as she held her hand out to me. "Come on, coven sister."

I took her hand and followed her through the trees, my smile just as big as hers. But she could not begin to understand my joy and my relief. Everything I ever lost had been returned to me.

She took me to a clearing where my future coven awaited. A large, white circle had been drawn on the ground in the middle. Laurel, the High Priestess stood in the center, wearing her ceremonial black robes with golden moons on them. All other coven members stayed outside the circle, standing around fires as they waited for the ceremony to begin.

Juno walked me to the edge of the circle, our arms linked together. I kept my eyes on Laurel but still noticed others in my peripheral vision. My grand-mother stood beaming with tears in her eyes. Far away from everyone else stood Ash with a handsome man

I'd never seen before, but the curling ram's horns growing from his forehead left few guesses as to his identity. No one else gave the impression that they could see either my demon or Lucifer himself.

"Who approaches this sacred space?" called Laurel in a booming voice that seemed to bounce off the surrounding hills.

"I bring you one who wishes to understand this coven, to honor the Goddess, the Horned God, Isis, Odin, and all of our sacred deities," Juno answered.

I stifled a smirk and kept my face neutral. How would any of them react if they knew Odin was just another one of Raum's identities?

"Seeker, by what name will you be known within this sacred circle?"

My original name played at my lips, but I answered with the one I was given in this lifetime.

"Deja."

"The gods have deemed you worthy," Laurel proclaimed. "Please enter the sacred circle and kneel in their presence."

Juno gave my hand a final squeeze as I stepped across the threshold. The air crackled and hummed with the coven's magic. I felt lightheaded as I kneeled, it was almost overwhelming.

"By joining this coven," Laurel said as she began walking a circle around me. "You become part of a greater spiritual family. As such, you are part of an endless circle of kinship and hospitality. Hail ye, Gods and Goddesses! Hail to kinsmen and clan, to the ancestors who watch over us, and to those who may follow. Here before you kneels Deja, the Seeker, soon to be a sworn part of this coven."

She walked around me counterclockwise three times, her fingers barely skimming over my shoulders, but the weight of her power was heavy and humbling.

"As a Dedicant of this coven, you will learn and grow and evolve every day. You will seek new knowledge, and attain it in direct proportion to your efforts. Let the Gods and the Ancient Ones guide you on your journey."

She stopped in front of me, tilting my chin to make eye contact with her. "Are you willing and able to uphold the values and principles of this coven?"

"Yes," I said as each of my three demons' faces cycled through my mind.

"Are you prepared, Deja, to be born anew, to begin this day a brand new journey, as part of your new spiritual family, and as a child of the Gods?"

"I am."

"Then rise, Deja, and emerge from the womb of darkness, and be welcomed into the light and love of the Gods. You are no longer a mere Seeker, but a Dedicant of this coven."

I stood to my feet while keeping my head bowed. Laurel placed a long chain over my head, on the end which hung a large, yellow moonstone pendant. The mineral of the Golden Moon Coven rested just below my sternum and seemed to vibrate with magic.

Laurel pulled me forward gently and kissed each of my cheeks.

"Welcome, Deja, to your new family," she beamed. "May you be blessed by the Gods."

She held up a robe, black with golden moons, and everyone cheered as I slid my arms through it.

The solemn ritual turned into a party in the blink of an eye. People whooped and laughed as they brought out coolers full of drinks from their cars and freshly hunted game to roast over the fires. As I drank and danced and hugged my new family members, I couldn't even believe that I spent most of this lifetime condemning this spiritual practice. The energy in the air was pure joy, kinship, and love. I knew I made the right decision by choosing this family for this brief lifetime.

It was a good half hour before I could sneak away to the edge of the clearing, where Ash and Lucifer calmly watched our celebrations.

"Congratulations, my dear," Lucifer said as he took my hand and placed a small kiss on the back of my palm. "It's good to have you back again."

"Thank you, my Lord," I said, lowering my eyes respectfully before turning to Ash.

My Ash. The one I saved and the one who saved me. My first and forever love.

He wore his usual cool expression but his eyes brimmed with anticipation.

"Tell me," he said, his voice thick with emotion. "Tell me your name from when we first met."

I grinned, my heart nearly bursting with the love I carried for him since the dawn of humanity itself.

"My name is Lilith, the first wife of Adam, consort of demons, and mother of all witches."

TO BE CONTINUED IN WITCH'S BETRAYAL:
BOOK 3 OF THE UNHOLY TRINITY SERIES

COMING JUNE 2018

KEEP READING FOR A SNEAK PREVIEW!

ABOUT THE AUTHOR

I love all things mysterious and unusual, so naturally I love paranormal, fantasy and reverse harem romance! You'll find a mixture of all these elements in my books.

When I'm not writing, you can find me mixing various tea and alcohol concoctions (sometimes successfully!), cooing at cute reptiles, or reading one of the thousands of books on my Kindle.

Thank you so much for reading Witch's Dawn! If you enjoyed it, I would be honored if you left a review.

Also get the **free** prequel to the Unholy Trinity series when you visit my website!

Get in touch with me!
crystalashbooks.com
authorcrystalash@gmail.com

ALSO BY CRYSTAL ASH

Unholy Trinity series

Her 3 Demons (free prequel)

Witch's Dawn

Witch's Betrayal (June 2018)

Witch's Exile (July 2018)

Witch's Rebirth (August 2018)

79099294R00092

Made in the USA
Middletown, DE
08 July 2018